"Foolish senhorita! You are afraid."

Laurel looked tearfully into the Conde's eyes. "Of course I'm afraid!" she cried. "You just tried to drown me and now you're trying to force me to go home with you. You must be crazy!"

"You don't know what you are saying," the Conde snapped, glints of impatience narrowing his dark eyes. "You will come home with me to recover from your hysteria."

"I'm not hysterical!" Laurel said wildly. "I just want to get away from this place—and you."

"We shall see." The Conde turned abruptly and strode away down the beach, his shadow falling sharp and black against the golden sand.

For some reason Laurel shivered and put her hand to her heart.

Other titles by

MARGERY HILTON
IN HARLEQUIN PRESENTS

Other titles by

MARGERY HILTON
IN HARLEQUIN ROMANCES

Many of these titles, and other titles in the Harlequin
Romance series, are available at your local
bookseller or through the Harlequin Reader Service.
For a free catalogue listing all available Harlequin
Presents and Harlequin Romances, send your name
and address to:

HARLEQUIN READER SERVICE,
M.P.O. Box 707,
Niagara Falls, N.Y. 14302
Canadian address:
Stratford, Ontario, Canada   N5A 6W2
or use coupon at back of book.

MARGERY HILTON

the velvet touch

Harlequin Books

TORONTO • LONDON • NEW YORK • AMSTERDAM
SYDNEY • HAMBURG • PARIS

Harlequin Presents edition published July 1979
ISBN 0-373-70797-5

Original hardcover edition published in 1979
by Mills & Boon Limited

CHAPTER ONE

THANK heaven it would soon be Saturday!

Laurel Daneway put the sheaf of notes on Mr Searle's desk, capped her machine with its cover, and turned the key of her drawer. Then she crossed her fingers and wished.

She was not an unduly superstitious girl, but the day was far from over, even though it was nearing seven and she should have been finished over an hour ago. She was beginning to wonder if indeed there were some potent malign being whose special day of joy was Friday the thirteenth. If there were, he had certainly had a field day today as far as Planet Panorama Holidays was concerned!

The boss called away by family trouble, the Rome courier gone sick, the opening of the new La Reina hotel delayed yet again by industrial action—where on earth were they going to transfer the three hundred hopefuls who had booked for the opening gala week? —and the lunch-time news to cap it all. A small war in Saringo, surely the last safe standby left on the globe, as far as arranging holidays was concerned. They hadn't had a war there since Hannibal crossed the Alps! And now there were forty-five trusting, highly nervous old dears marooned there in the middle of it.

It made Laurel feel that her own tribulations, like a tear in her tights, missing the bus that morning, and being stood up for the weekend, were petty worries in comparison. It had also made her muttered imprecations concerning a missing boss rather uncharitable. After all, he was really a darling to work for, and all the bad news would be waiting for him in the morning ...

A frown puckered Laurel's brow as she glanced round the office before letting herself out. Had she

5

done the right thing in sending Jeanne off by the evening flight to Rome? And phoning Roy in Tangier to tell him to leave everything to his assistant and get himself into Saringo come hell or high water to look after those forty-five very precious clients ...? She did not usually have to make such vital decisions, but there had been no one else available.

The phone began to shrill as she snapped the door shut. She sighed softly, standing indecisively in the corridor while the imperative summons went on behind the closed door, then quickly fished out her key to re-open the office. She ran now, braced for another crisis and half expecting the phone to go silent before she could reach it. Unless Phil had found he was free tonight after all.

But it wasn't Phil; it was her boss.

He spoke quickly, seeming not to hear the drop of disappointment she could not keep out of her voice, and brushing aside the account of disasters she would have launched into he said: 'Are you free? Could you get over here by eight?'

'I think so.' She stared at the calendar on the wall, her frown deepening. What did Mr Searle want to discuss with her that was so important?

'Don't bother trying to rush home to change,' he instructed dryly, after telling her where to meet him for the meal. It was as though he sensed her dismayed mental picture of herself. 'I know you won't believe me,' he went on, 'but you always manage to look as attractive when you leave the office as when you walk in bandbox-fresh in the morning.'

'Thank you,' she said, knowing that Gordon Searle didn't indulge in idle compliments for the sake of them. 'But ...?'

'I'm sorry to spring this on you,' he sighed, 'but I need your help, Laurie. Rather badly. Can you get round as quickly as possible? Take a taxi. Okay?'

'Yes, of course, Mr Searle.' Somewhat mystified, she rang off, then dialled their taxi service. While she waited she hurriedly touched up her make-up and swept her long, silver-gilt hair back into a smooth chignon. Whatever had happened? He sounded so worried, and usually he was quite unflappable.

He was waiting for her at the restaurant, and his smile was courteous as ever, but she noticed the drawn look round his eyes. Was his wife ill again? Or his daughter rebelling again? Could the firm be in financial difficulties?

She had to wait until they were settled at an alcove table, the order given and aperitifs brought, before he dropped the façade of sociality and looked directly at her across the table.

'I meant to leave this until Monday,' he began, 'but unfortunately my domestic affairs have reached crisis point and I've had to change my plans.'

Laurel sipped her Campari and nodded, waiting for him to go on.

'You'll remember my mentioning the possibility of our opening out a new island venue? There are two possible starters: Maraxos in the Ionian group, and Destino, a tiny spot north of but not belonging to the Canaries. I've just got a preliminary report on Maraxos, and I was planning to go out to Destino next week to look at it myself.'

Their first course arrived at that moment, and Gordon Searle waited until they were alone again before he resumed his explanation. A sudden warmth of enthusiasm temporarily drove the worry out of his expression as he outlined his plans for a new cruise-and-stay package the firm would offer the following year. Then he checked himself and smiled wryly.

'You're probably wondering why on earth I dragged you out tonight to tell you this. But unfortunately I'm not going to make it next week, so I want you to go in my place.'

'Me?' Laurel stopped eating. 'You mean to this island?'

He nodded. 'And make a report on it.'

'But I'm only your secretary,' she exclaimed. 'I—I

wouldn't have the first idea of judging its suitability.
I'd——'

'You'd do extremely well,' he broke in firmly. 'It's
only a preliminary survey. Checking some facts. Making
a reconnaissance and noting the things that would
worry you during a holiday. In fact, that's what you will
be doing, and depending on your report I'll follow it
up. Find out about treacherous currents—poor beaches
and unsafe bathing are no good to us. Talk to the
locals, find out the snags and sound opinion about
tourism. The main thing is that you remain incognito.
We don't want our rivals on the scene, and the less anyone knows of our plans at this stage, especially on the
island itself, the better.'

He looked at her hopefully, and the worried lines
had gathered round his eyes again. She said doubtfully,
'You know I'd do anything to help, but I'd hate to
make a mess of things.'

'You won't. How could you? There isn't much in
the way of accommodation, I'm afraid. Only one small
place that takes in about half a dozen people. It's run
by a retired English couple who've lived there several
years. From all accounts it's the same old story; in-
flation, and a pension that no longer supports them
adequately, so they boost their income with a few
guests during the season. Very quiet, middle-class sort
of simplicity. A chap at my club put me on to this. Says
it's totally unspoilt, almost feudal, but he seemed a bit
dubious about the water supply. So you'd have to find
out about that. The plan's off if the water supply dries
up after the first day of spring sunshine.'

Laurel was silent. She wished she could summon up
the same confidence in her own ability to make this
vital assessment as Gordon Searle seemed to have. How
did a girl, a stranger in the place, discover the vagaries
of its water sources? And what was the language?
Spanish or Portuguese? Not that it mattered, as she
couldn't speak a word of either.

He said slowly, 'I've already made a provisional

booking for you, for a month, but I feel it's only fair to tell you, before you commit yourself, that there are two snags.'

She smiled faintly. 'Tell me the worst.'

'I want you to take my daughter with you.'

'Yvonne!' Laurel had a vivid mental picture of the spoilt, self-willed sixteen-year-old who was a constant source of worry to her father. 'Does she want to see the island?' she asked aloud.

'It's the last thing in the world she wants at this moment,' he said grimly, 'but frankly, I'm at my wits' end over that brat. My wife's anything but well just now, and Yvonne's latest is guaranteed to wreck her health completely.'

'I'm sorry,' said Laurel, genuine sympathy in her grey eyes. 'Of course I'll do whatever I can to help.'

'I know, and I appreciate that very much, my dear,' he said heavily, 'but if you are to understand I must take you into my confidence. I know you'll be discreet.'

She felt a quickening of curiosity that was perfectly natural, but she nodded and met his gaze seriously.

'Yvonne has got herself mixed up with some undesirables, one boy in particular. We've tried reasoning with her, we've tried threats, and we've tried bribes.' He sighed and shook his head tiredly. 'But she refuses to listen. And now I've been warned that this boy is mixed up with the drug scene. I've *got* to get Yvonne away. It would break her mother's heart if she knew, and if Yvonne got involved . . .'

He stopped, reaching for his wine glass, and Laurel's own imagination had no difficulty in filling in the unspoken fear that haunted his eyes.

After a moment he said slowly: 'This morning I gave her the choice; to go with you, ostensibly to help you— which she won't, of course, but I thought it might appeal to her vanity. Or I'd stop her allowance till the end of the year.' He gave a grim smile. 'She settled for the holiday. Yvonne likes her comfort, and I think she's shrewd enough to realise that I've passed the stage of making idle threats. I'm afraid it's not exactly an auspicious prospect, from your point of view. Am I asking too much of you?'

Ten minutes previously Laurel might have expressed her doubts, but now she was committed emotionally. Her sympathies were aroused, and the generous instincts which had often in the past caused her to take on other people's problems without pausing to consider the extent she might become involved herself.

'No, of course not,' she said impulsively. 'And please try not to worry too much—I'm sure it'll work out—for Yvonne, I mean. After a month's holiday she may see this boy in a different light altogether, her own good sense should make her realise she's been a bit silly, and if you're understanding, let her see that you realise how easy it is to be taken in by someone who isn't what they seem, I'm sure she'll meet you halfway.'

'I hope you're right.' Gordon Searle gave a sigh, then straightened his shoulders. 'But I feel I have to warn you that she may prove difficult. If the worst comes, you'll have to contact me and let her come home. You can't keep a self-willed teenager anywhere against her will these days.'

Laurel knew this was only too true. If Yvonne decided she had had enough of Destino there would be little she could do about it, other than send her home to her despairing parents. But surely Yvonne wasn't as awkward as all that. If she was in love with this boy it was very unlikely that she would see him in the same sinister light as her father.

'If possible, I should like you to travel on the first —that's next Friday. If——'

Laurel must have given a tiny gasp of dismay, for he stopped and looked questioningly at her. 'Is that inconvenient?'

'No.' She hesitated only a fraction of a second, steeling her heart against the thought of the weekend that might be spent with Phil. She had been foolish too long, keeping all her time free for Phil, avoiding making arrangements a while in advance in case he suddenly rang up to say he was in town and where were they going ... Just as she could understand how Yvonne might feel, so should she recognise her own weakness ...

Her employer was looking rueful. 'I'm sorry, my dear. I've been so wrapped up in my own worries I forgot about the fact that you have a personal life, and a young man who isn't going to take·very kindly to my removing you out of his reach for a whole month. Perhaps I'd better try and make other arrangements.'

'No, I'll go.' Laurel returned his gaze steadily. 'I'd like to. By the way,' she hurried on, 'I haven't told you about today ...' Quickly, her eyes becoming a little anxious, she recounted the chronicle of disasters, and ended: 'I hope I did the right thing, but I couldn't get in touch with you.'

Gordon Searle smiled whimsically. 'You did exactly what I would have done. Sent a replacement, and contacted Roy, asking him to leave his assistant courier in charge and go and sort out the Saringo problem.'

'Because this was Linda Dale's first job with the Saringo tour and she must be petrified with this happening.'

Gordon Searle nodded. 'Actually I did hear the news, and phoned Roy myself, but you'd already done that. And just before you arrived here tonight I was in touch with the Saringian authorities. They think they're containing the rebellion, and so far things are still quiet in the coastal province of Lyssan, where our party should be today, if they're on schedule—and there's no reason why they shouldn't be,' he added hopefully. 'So I'm hoping to hear later tonight that they'll be on their way out within a few hours.'

Laurel gave a sigh of relief. She sipped at her cooling coffee and thought of the job which lay ahead. Could she cope with this new responsibility thrust on her shoulders? For undoubtedly it was no light venture. On her report could depend the success and happiness of thousands of future holidays, to say nothing of the firm and the loss it might suffer if she made a mistake. And then there was Yvonne.

Suddenly she remembered something, and became aware of her employer regarding her with serious eyes.

He nodded. 'Yes, there's something else. The local lord of the manor—or his Spanish equivalent.'

'The second snag?'

'I'm afraid so.' Gordon Searle sighed. 'His estate covers a good two-thirds of the island, in effect, its most attractive area, I'm told. Apparently it's only one of lord knows how many he owns. There again, you may be able to sound local opinion and see if you can estimate the kind of reaction we're liable to meet from the gentleman. For a great deal will depend on his co-operation, and his attitude towards the island becoming a tourist centre.'

'You don't want me to go and see him?'

'Not until we've made this preliminary reconnaissance. We'd only waste his time and our own by contacting him before we're ready to make our decision.'

Laurel nodded thoughtfully. Already she was beginning to experience a sense of excitement. She had never done anything like this before, even the prospect of Yvonne proving a handful could not damp her eagerness, or the unknown quantity of the lord of this island domain. She said almost flippantly: 'You expect him to spell trouble?'

Gordon Searle hesitated, then nodded.

'Any special reason?' Laurel sobered, wondering why he hesitated.

'No, only my instinct.' Gordon Searle tugged at his lip. 'Unfortunately, or fortunately, I'm not often wrong.'

'What is his name—this island grandee?' she asked.

'I can't remember. I've got it written down somewhere. It's one of those long family strings—you know how their aristocracy often take on both names and estate title when two big families intermarry.'

Laurel didn't, but she murmured agreement as her

employer dug into his pocket for his wallet. He riffled through it and gave a small exclamation of triumph as he extracted an envelope. He straightened out its creases.

'Conde Vicente Rodrigo de Renzi y Valdes!' he proclaimed dramatically. He looked at her wide eyes and his mouth compressed wryly. 'He could be as great a problem as my daughter! But for your sake, my dear, I sincerely hope not.'

'So do I,' breathed Laurel.

But she had little time for much metaphorical crossing of bridges during the next few days. There were two newcomers to the staff at the office, which meant a certain amount of time had to be spent helping them to devise a routine which would cover her absence. Gordon Searle's wife learned that she would have to go into hospital for a minor operation as soon as this could be arranged, and while there wasn't any frightening urgency about it, nevertheless it was worrying for Laurel's employer, who was devoted to his delicate wife. Despite this, he did not forget what might have seemed less vital points to a man and insisted on making a generous expense allowance to Laurel to cover the cost of the additional clothes she would need.

'Nonsense,' he said, when she protested. 'You'll need suitable gear, and I've no intention of letting you stand the cost of clothes you wouldn't otherwise be buying.'

'But you're already paying me all expenses plus my salary,' she exclaimed.

'I'm claiming all your time, my dear,' he said firmly, 'besides landing you with Yvonne. And you should see the stuff she's bought for the trip,' he added feelingly. 'It looks enough to dress the entire Palladium troupe!'

So she spent a pleasant if hectic morning choosing beach wear and casual separates that would interchange. Mr Searle had warned her that shopping facilities were very limited on Destino, so she also bought supplies of sun lotion, films, and various other holiday needs.

On the Thursday morning Mr Searle brought

Yvonne along to the office and took the two girls out
to lunch. Yvonne, younger by four years, was tall for
her age, and Laurel felt quite small when her own five
foot four inches were ranged against Yvonne's five foot
seven. Yvonne was very attractive, she decided, with her
long lustrous raven-dark hair and vivid colouring, even
though petulance marred her full crimson mouth and
her attitude of resentment towards her father was
scarcely hidden. But youthful impetuosity began to
show through as the meal progressed, and Yvonne could
not resist detailing the new gear she had bought. She
described the long crimson voile skirt and tight white
lace top she'd bought for evening—'even though he'
—with an impertinent inclination of her head towards
her father—'says there isn't any night life and the place
we're staying isn't even a proper hotel. But it's ab-
solutely gorgeous and you can *just* see my legs through
it. I've got a tiny black velvet bolero to wear with it. I
shall look like a *señorita*!'

'You'll be run off the island if you wear a semi-
transparent skirt without a petticoat underneath,'
Gordon Searle told his daughter patiently.

'Petticoat!' Scorn curled Yvonne's red mouth.
'There'd be a slip attached to it if the designer thought
it necessary. And if anyone objects I shan't be staying
long enough to be run off their lousy island. It sounds
like the last place God made, anyway. Don't you think
so?'

Appealed to, Laurel could only shake her head and
smile. 'We can't judge until we get there. And the sun
will be the super attraction, being able to wear our
swimsuits all day if we want to.'

Yvonne looked at the grey drizzle outside the restaurant window and conceded the point. Although April
was nearly gone it had left spring far behind somewhere along the way, and there was little temptation
by the weather to do much blossoming out in summer
finery.

Laurel parted on reasonably amiable terms with her
future charge, and spent the afternoon with her em-

ployer going over her schedule for collecting the information he required. After a tray of tea and sandwiches in the office he wished her luck and sent her home to get her packing and personal chores done. By eight o'clock she was exhausted. She had completed her packing, tidied the flat, left a month's rent with her friend in the downstairs flatlet, remembered to leave a note to stop the milk, and all that remained to do was have a shampoo and bath. They were leaving on an early flight so she must not risk sleeping in and not being ready when her boss called to collect her and drive her to the airport.

She was running the water into the bath when the door bell rang.

Giving a muttered exclamation of dismay, she clutched her wrap about her and went to open the door a few cautious inches. The man waiting impatiently outside stepped forward, his smile coming with easy self-assurance, then his eyes rounded and he gave a soft, appreciative whistle.

'Phil!' she gasped, torn between dismay and delight. 'But I didn't——'

'Not to worry, darling. I don't mind waiting.' He was stepping across the threshold, utterly confident of his welcome, and his hands were reaching for her. 'After all, we did have a date, didn't we?'

'Yes, but . . .' Laurel disengaged herself rather quickly from his embrace, suddenly conscious of her somewhat inadequate attire and a certain emphasised warmth about his kiss. She gestured helplessly. 'But I didn't expect you—you rang to say you were tied up all this week, so——'

'I know, darling.' His whimsical mouth, the brown eyes widened ruefully, and contrite voice all expressed the charm she'd never been able to resist from the first moment he walked into her life six months ago. 'But fortunately I was able to clear up this tiresome business with Daverley's quicker than I'd expected, and then Jake Harving rang to say that tomorrow's conference was off because he had to go up to our northern factory to sort out a spot of bother there. So I'm free! All yours until Monday morning, sweetie.'

He kissed her startled mouth lightly and moved across the living room. He stopped at the little cupboard where she kept her modest store of refreshment, and slid the glass door along. Perfectly at home, he frowned at the sherry bottle that was less than half full, and held up the bottle of Martini.

'Lovey, we *are* well down below the plimsoll line. Or have you a new cellar hidden away somewhere?'

He was getting two glasses out as he spoke, and when she made no immediate response he swung round. 'Darling, don't just stand there. It's after nine, you know. So go and brush out those lovely locks and get ready, there's a good girl. Unless,' his mouth pursed appreciatively, 'that's your latest in hostess gowns and you'd rather make it an at-home tonight. It's okay by me!'

'No—it isn't, and I wouldn't.' She tightened the sash about her waist and pulled the lace fronts of her wrap primly up to her throat. 'Phil, I can't go out with you. I was just running a bath, and my hair's still wet. I'm——'

'What do you mean? You can't.' He put the glasses down and moved forward swiftly. 'All right, I know. You're piqued, my darling.' He put placating hands on her shoulders and looked down into her eyes. 'So let me make a very special apology—but I couldn't help it, you know.'

'You said that the last time, and the time before.' Laurel was aware of tiredness, and a sad little stab of disillusion that she was beginning to recognise Phil's winning line in blarney. 'It's too late. I have to be up very early tomorrow because——'

'Tomorrow! But there's all tonight first! Come on, Laurie,' he put a finger under her chin and smiled, 'kiss and make up, then we'll go on the town. Anywhere you like! How about——?'

'No!' Almost despairingly she eluded another embrace, knowing how difficult it was to resist Phil when he chose to exert his most persuasive charm. 'I can't, Phil. I'm going away tomorrow.'

'Away?' The smile died from his handsome face and a frown flickered across his dark brow. 'What do you mean? You're going away? You never said anything about this,' he exclaimed, almost accusingly.

'I didn't know myself till last weekend,' she told him, giving a small shake of her head. 'You've been away all week. How could I let you know?'

His mouth tightened with a brief flash of petulance as he seemed to realise that she stated only a fact. Then he said slowly, 'Yes, of course ... But isn't it all very sudden? How long?'

'A month, perhaps longer. You see——'

'A month!' he echoed, aghast. 'Oh, no, Laurie, you can't do this to me. It'll ruin everything.' He stared at her bewildered expression, then hurried on: 'Listen, we've been invited to Jake Harving's place next week-end—down near Hove. This is the first time I've had an invite to one of Jake's weekend do's. Oh, Laurie! you've got to get back in time.'

Laurel bit her lip. 'But I can't. Everything's fixed. Besides, I don't know Mr Harving. Why has he asked me? I mean, if it's a business affair ...'

'No, you don't understand,' he said, almost desperately. 'This is a tremendous chance for me. I'll be meeting influential people, and it means that Jake is beginning to recognise my potential—he never admits junior execs into his social life unless he's pretty impressed with them. But naturally he usually invites one to bring a girl, if one isn't married. And naturally I thought of you, never dreaming that anything like this would happen.'

Laurel sighed. 'I'm sorry, Phil, but I don't see what I can do. My trip is business too, and I've given my word.' She shrugged helplessly. 'I can't let Mr Searle down. But I'll willingly send my apologies to your boss —even though the invitation didn't come personally— if you think that'll help.'

'You still don't understand,' he repeated impatiently.

'I've talked about you, and Jake expressed a wish to meet you. You're the kind of girl he'd like. You dress beautifully, and you mix so easily. You always seem right, you *are* right, in every way, and that's of importance to someone like Jake. And now you stand there and tell me you can't make it. You're going away —just like that!'

He was too wrapped up in his own indignation to notice the danger sign beginning to sparkle in Laurel's eyes. When he stopped and looked at her as though he expected instant contrition, her temper flared.

'Listen, Phil. I've said I'm sorry, and that's the end of it. I'm certainly not going to start altering my plans at this late hour just to keep what amounts to a casual invitation to a weekend party from a man I've never met, even if he is your boss. Anyway,' she gestured, 'I still fail to see how my not being there is going to have any effect on your future chances of promotion.'

'Do you? Then it's time you did,' he said bitterly. 'The right woman in a man's background can make all the difference in the world in some companies; and ours is one of them. I thought I mattered to you,' he said through tight lips, 'but apparently I don't.'

For a moment Laurel was speechless as the full implication of Phil's words got home. Then she took a deep breath, controlling her temper with difficulty while she said quietly: 'You did matter to me. If it's any consolation, I fell in love with you the very first time you took me out. But it seems you weren't looking for a girl to fall in love with yourself, even for friendly companionship. You were looking for an asset, for a girl who looked right.' Laurel's voice rose sharply with bitterness and scorn. 'You wanted a girl of whom your boss would approve. A girl who would fit in with what *he* deemed a suitable feminine background for his junior executives. Well, I'm not that girl.'

Slowly she crossed to the door and opened it, a curiously appealing and dignified air about her, despite the damp tendrils of hair curling about her brow, and the soft flowing folds of blue housecoat clinging to her

slender figure. 'I don't think there's anything else to
say, Phil . . .'

She waited, while he stared at her with incredulous
eyes. He took a step forward. 'You—you don't mean
this, Laurie. You can't.'

'Oh, but I do.'

'But we're in love with each other! You've admitted
it. And I can soon prove it.' He moved towards her
with purposeful steps, his intent obvious.

'No.' She put up her hands to ward off his embrace,
keeping her expression cold. She knew of the power
Phil held to stir her senses, should she be unwary
enough to allow him the chance to use it, and the cold
hard core of logic in her brain warned her not to
weaken. 'I'm tired of standing by, waiting for the phone
to ring, listening to your excuses, being available whenever it suited *your* book. It's over, Phil. I mean it.'

'I believe you do.' But he seemed unbelieving as he
stood there. 'And to think I believed you understood,
that I was working for us, for our future. That as soon
as I'd carved out a secure niche for myself in the firm
I'd be able to offer you marriage, and the kind of home
we could both be proud of. You're making a terrible
mistake, Laurie.'

She shook her head. All the things she'd tried to
shut her eyes to were revealed with stark clarity. That
basically Phil was selfish; that any girl who gave her
heart to him would have to learn to subject her life
totally to him. That what Phil wanted in life would
always come first, and that the sweet charm would
soon be revealed as the sham of excuses for that very
selfishness. Ambition was all very well, and perhaps
there were many girls who would disagree with her, but
Laurel wanted more than that from the man she would
choose as her life partner. Last of all did she want to
be chosen because she was the kind of girl who would
come out with a top score from the boss's vetting.

She looked at him, an infinite sadness in her eyes as
she recognised yet another truth; that even now Phil
was acting. The smooth glib phrases came off his

tongue so easily, the hurt, badly-done-to expression that drooped around his mouth even as the hint of suppressed anger darkened his eyes.

For a moment she thought he would argue further, but he changed his mind and gave a shrug that plainly expressed resignation.

'I can see I'm wasting my time talking to you while you're in this frame of mind,' he said sulkily. 'Perhaps you'll think differently later. Goodnight, Laurel.'

Which meant he might be prepared to forgive her, later on, when she came to her senses and made apologies which he considered adequate and fitting, she thought bitterly. But she remained silent and unmoved, except for a toneless little goodnight, after which he closed the door with a suspicion of a snap.

She heard his sharp footsteps diminish in sound as he went down the stairs, and then the slam of the outer door. Only then did she turn back to the silent room, and the full comprehension of what she had done.

She willed herself to complete the tasks he had interrupted, determined not to allow herself to descend into useless regret. For it was over; she had to face that fact. For unless she made the first move Phil would never come back. She had hurt his pride, even as she had denied her own heart. But better to recognise the truth now, than later, when the anguish would be infinitely more severe.

Despite all her resolution she cried that night, once the little lamp was extinguished and darkness crowded about her. She lay awake for long hours, wishing he hadn't come, that it wasn't all over, that Jake Harving hadn't issued that invitation. What had he said? *Bring that girl of yours along. Let's have a look at her . . .?* Or had it been couched in more man-of-the-world terms?

Laurel sighed into her pillow. She would never know, but somehow the scene with Phil seemed a daunting omen for the future. She remembered Gordon Searle's warning, and she thought of Yvonne, and wondered uneasily about the unknown quantity of the local lord of the manor—if that were the proper term for a Latin grandee who sounded anything but welcoming. Was she going to be able to cope with the problems awaiting her?

Suddenly she felt alone and forlorn, and just a little afraid ...

CHAPTER TWO

'OH, leave me alone! I can't be bothered!' Yvonne flounced across to the big garden swing and hurled herself into it, glowering petulantly at Laurel.

Laurel looked down uneasily at the slender young figure in its briefest of orange-flowered bikinis and felt dismay. This was it, the start of the rebellion about which her employer had warned her and which she had sensed was simmering in the spoilt daughter of Gordon Searle ever since the moment they arrived at the Villa Cristina.

Yvonne glanced up with scarcely veiled insolence. 'You're wasting your time standing there. I'm not coming with you.'

Laurel restrained impatience. Yvonne had been unusually quiet over breakfast and there was the possibility that she was suffering a reaction to too much sun and the change of food. She said quietly: 'You're not feeling off-colour or anything, Yvonne?'

'Ha ha! Everybody laugh!' Yvonne stabbed viciously at the ground with a white-sandalled foot, sending the canopied swing into a violent motion that narrowly missed Laurel. 'Oh, yes, there's something the matter with me! I'm bored! Bored to extinction. We've been here three days, and all we've done is walk! Walk round this dreary island. There's nothing to do, nowhere to go, and nothing to see when you get there. Island of Destiny!' she added disgustedly. 'I could tell you what its destiny ought to be. It ought to——'

'Keep your voice down,' Laurel said sharply. 'Be fair, Yvonne, you knew there wouldn't be many tourists and it would be quiet.'

'Quiet!' Yvonne exploded. 'It's so quiet you can hear the cabbages growing. As for tourists ...! There are eight people in this—this apology for an hotel, and I think I'm the only one without one foot in the grave. There's old Colonel Carlton and his wife doddering about. He talks politics all day and she bleats about what's wrong with the young people today. I could tell her what's wrong with her generation. And Mr Binkley, silly old fool, trying to pinch my bottom when he thinks nobody's looking. He must be eighty if he's a day.'

'I haven't exactly got one foot in the grave,' Laurel said dryly.

'You're a female,' said Yvonne, as though this fact was somehow Laurel's fault. 'And then having that boring Miss Jessops tagging on to us yesterday, yackety-yacking all the time about the cost of living and how she can't afford to go to Cannes these days.'

Laurel sighed deeply. 'Miss Jessops is lonely. Her companion died recently and she's alone in the world now. It isn't much to give her, a few hours of companionship.'

'Not mine, thank you. Why doesn't she get herself another companion, someone as dried up and dull as herself, if she's that lonely?'

Laurel came perilously near to losing her temper. 'Listen,' she said grimly, 'I know it's quiet. I know there aren't any young people here at the moment, but try to remember that I happen to be here to do a job—a job for which your father is paying me.'

'Nobody's stopping you doing your job.' Yvonne gave another petulant thrust to set the swing going again. 'All I'm asking is that you leave me out of it.'

'But what will you do on your own?'

'I'll find something to do, I suppose. Go for a swim, then read, maybe.' Yvonne fished her sunglasses out of her tote bag and donned them. 'But I'm not going tramping for miles. I got a blister yesterday, *if* you remember.'

'Yes, but you wouldn't have had that if you hadn't insisted on wearing unsuitable shoes.'

'I like those shoes, and I bought them especially for the trip.'

Laurel looked at her despairingly. She was rapidly discovering the difficulty of winning an argument, no matter how logically, with the self-willed Yvonne. But what could she do? She had her job to do, and she had undertaken to look after her unwilling charge, who plainly had no intention of setting forth on another exploratory ramble over Destino's beautiful, unspoilt countryside. Laurel made a final attempt at persuasion.

'Well, I think it's fun exploring a strange island. I'm enjoying it. And you must admit that the scenery is beautiful.'

'Nobody's stopping you enjoying it.' Yvonne waved her hand. 'I'm not,' she added pointedly.

At that moment Rosita, the little maid, came across the garden. She was carrying a small basket.

'Your picnic lunch, *señoritas*.' She handed the basket to Laurel and went on her way towards the kitchen garden, which lay to the rear of the long, low white villa.

Laurel stood indecisively, watching the slim, black-clad form of the Spanish girl pass through the high, scrolled iron gate in the wall. Through its lacelike pattern she glimpsed another figure, that of Renaldo, the Latin-dark young waiter whose velvet eyes and melting smile enchanted the elderly female guests each day in the dining room, if not the male diners. Colonel Carlton had been heard to refer to him as another of those confounded dagoes, while Mr Binkley was equally disapproving and unable to understand why, in a guest house run by British proprietors, they couldn't employ British staff who understood plain English. Laurel's lips curved wryly at the fleeting thought then parted in a smile as there was a slight flurry of activity beyond the tall gate. The small feminine squeal and giggle was undoubtedly from Rosita, as was the protest which followed, to be abruptly silenced for a few moments before Rosita emerged, tossing her dark hair across her shoulder as she marched back into the house. The gate clanged, and Laurel came back to her own problem.

'What about your lunch—I told them we'd both be

out all day?' She gestured to the basket. 'It's in here.'

'So what?' Yvonne yawned. 'I shan't starve, don't worry.'

'No, I don't suppose you will.' Laurel's mouth tightened. 'I suppose I'd better find Mrs Allen and explain.'

'I'll do that.' Yvonne gave an unexpectedly winsome smile. 'I've got a tongue in my head, you know. She won't mind if I talk to her nicely.'

'You're hopeless!' Laurel decided to give it up. 'Don't forget to apologise—and don't go swimming straight after food, do you hear?'

'I promise.' Yvonne pretended to cross her heart. 'Now hadn't you better get a move on? It's going to be too hot to move before you get anywhere.'

After a moment or so of hesitation Laurel tucked her map into the basket and donned her sunglasses. She was experiencing prickles of unease regarding Yvonne for which she could find no logical reason. After all, what harm could befall Yvonne, short of drowning herself or falling off the cliff or something equally unlikely? And what could she do about the matter, short of forcibly tipping the rebellious Yvonne out of the swing and insisting on obedience? A course of action unlikely to have much success, Laurel told herself as she turned away at last and let herself out of the side door in the high wall.

She set off up the narrow path that wound its tortuous way up the hillside. The previous afternoon she had noticed a second path forking from it about halfway to the summit, and today she intended to explore it and add its contours to the rough map she was trying to make of the island. Perhaps it would lead to the far end of the island, hidden beyond the second ridge of hills which crossed Destino. Perhaps it would lead her to that great sun-washed shape of the *castillo* that dominated the island.

What was it like? And its daunting grandee owner?

But she wasn't here to speculate—or gatecrash. Her folder was already filling with notes, and she was beginning to think that Mr Searle could be on to a winner.

Admittedly there was a debit of material amusements,
as Yvonne had disgustedly noticed, but for a rugged,
outdoor holiday Destino had much to commend it. Hot
sun, with sea winds to temper the heat. Safe bathing
from a glorious beach within minutes of the guest
house, and on the sheltered side, away from the great
Atlantic breakers that could make sea bathing impossible on the exposed western coast. There were groves
and ravines to ramble through inland, hills to climb
to see fantastic views, and a picturesque village where
the women sat by their doorways working at exquisitely
stitched embroidery. The local wine was cheap and
good, there was an abundance of fruit, the seafood was
superb, and the fresh sweet air held its own heady
bouquet. But it still remained for Laurel to discover
the practical facts about water supplies and if there
were suitable sites likely to be available for building.
For she had seen little sign so far of premises that
promised more wide-scale accommodation. Perhaps on
the far side of the island . . .

The path wound its way round the gentle curve of
the hill, eventually coming out above the terraced
slopes and lush dark groves that stretched into the
distance to where the second line of hills rose to the
skyline. These would be the citrus groves, which, along
with the rich dark Destino wine that held such an
unsuspected bite and potency, provided the island with
its principal exports. The vineyards lay on the far side
of those second hills, rather too distant to reach on
foot from Laurel's starting point at the guest house,
but she intended to try to reach them today, which
was why she had set out prepared with a picnic lunch as
it would be very late by the time she got back at night.

By eleven she judged she had covered almost half of
the distance, although the rugged green slopes looked
as far distant as ever. She perched on a sun-warmed out-
crop of rock, allowing herself ten minutes' rest and the
refreshment of an apple before she moved on. It was
almost one o'clock, and the sun reaching its hottest, by
the time she found herself at the end of the path. It met

another, leading up into the hills on her right, and on her left led down towards a small sandy bay sheltered by rocky cliffs. Without pausing to ponder any decision she turned thankfully downhill towards the sea.

The beach was deserted. Laurel found a suitable hollow and settled herself comfortably. She opened her lunch basket and spread out her repast on the cloth Mrs Allen had thoughtfully included. It was incredibly quiet, and Laurel began to get the feeling that she was the only being alive. Somehow it was difficult to believe that anyone lived within miles of this wild, remote little cove on whose clean, sea-washed sands only her own footprints showed. No transistors, no beach balls flying, no voices of excited children or the scampering paws of dogs. This was away from it all with a vengeance. Perfect for lovers!

The sun made her drowsy, and she lay back for a while, closing her eyes against the glare but not sleeping, conscience telling her she must not linger too long; she had a job to do. When at last she sat up she found she had lain there in a bemused calm for well over an hour. She found that she was also very hot, very sticky, and her limbs evinced not the slightest inclination to obey the command of duty that said get up and go. Sighing, she stowed away the remains of her lunch, closed the basket, and stared at the sea. It had never looked more inviting.

She took off her sensible canvas shoes which, while they were more suitable than sandals, had still not saved her feet from feeling the effects of all the walking she had done, and ran down to the edge of the sea. It was bliss! She played tag with the ripples for a while, then returned to where her things lay. If only she had brought swim things!

She sighed again, brushing sand from her toes, then the outrageous temptation came. Dared she? Just a brief dip, just to freshen herself?

She looked round, temptation and inhibition battling in her. There was no one in sight and she could see every nook of this rocky little cove enclosed within high slopes which ended in two low headlands stretching out into the sea. The path leading down to it was empty and there wasn't a sign of a house for miles—except for that great *castillo* up there, and it was always there! No, this was obviously a lonely, unfrequented part of the island. She looked up at the *castillo*—did they sit around with binoculars?—and then at those gorgeous cascading ripples, and yielded. Anyway, it was siesta time! Who would be awake to see her at the high noon of the day?

In moments she had slipped free of her denim pants and cotton shirt, tucked her briefs and bra into a tight little bundle with them, and fled into the cover of the waves.

It was heavenly!

She swam leisurely along, parallel with the beach, revelling in the silken swish of the water against her body and telling herself she would stay in for only a few minutes, just long enough to cool and refresh herself ...

But the sun was hot, the sky a rich heavenly blue, and this was the first time Laurel had ever swum in the nude; she had never dreamed how pleasurable and exhilarating an experience it could be. She forgot time, forgot everything except this newfound joyous freedom, and frolicked in the water as she had not done since childhood. Once she had been able to turn a somersault ... could she still ...? And a dozen strokes underwater ...? Somewhat to her surprise she could, and she came up spluttering and laughing with sheer happiness.

Tired at last, she floated, and remembering, looked towards the shore, suddenly anxious. But her basket and the little bundle of clothing lay exactly as she had left them, and there was no one to be seen. Too late she realised she had no towel, but she pushed away the rueful thought; there were some paper towels in her bag that would mop up the rivulets, and a cotton bandana she could wring out her hair with. She would soon dry off in this heat! She turned over to begin her swim ashore, and almost fainted with shock. She was no longer alone.

Someone was swimming towards her, cleaving the water with long, effortless strokes that lessened the distance to half in the few seconds it took for her to comprehend the awful truth.

It was a man!

Laurel's mouth opened, inadvertently admitting quite an amount of the Atlantic, and she went under. Panic welling, she came up gasping and turned to escape in the only direction left, out to sea.

'Señora!—Señorita!'

The deep sharp voice rang across the blue. Laurel quickened her stroke. Where on earth had he sprung from? Why had he had to materialise now? Or had he observed her earlier on? With the result that she was now about to collect a young Latin hotblood who had decided she was fair game ... Laurel snatched another glance back and her worst suspicion was realised: he *was* following her!

'Pare! Señorita—tenga cuidado!'

Stop! Not likely! How could she? Laurel ploughed on wildly, praying her pursuer would weary and give up, but a fresh torrent of Spanish rang across the water. He must have lungs and stamina of steel! He was very near now, and through blurs of wetness she glimpsed powerful arms cutting the blue. Laurel ceased her frantic strokes, summoning breath to cry out a desperate appeal:

'Go away—please!'

'Por Dios! Una inglesa—I might have known!'

The fierce response ricocheted across the swirling ripples and Laurel ducked frantically, forcing her tired limbs back to action. It was years since she'd swum at this clip. Was the man crazy? She must have come miles out. How was she going to make it back? And the water was so cold now, rougher.

She strove not to surrender to panic, feverishly wondering which was the lesser fate; to perish from sheer

exhaustion in a sea no longer so benign and blue, or be
caught swimming nude by a mad, determined Latin
bent on—what was he bent on, anyway? Laurel's brain
went blank and everything fled before the sheer pain
that seized her leg and seemed to radiate through her
entire body. She spun helplessly, not knowing what had
happened, then with a choked cry she went under,
caught in the nightmare that strikes without warning.
Cramp!

She came to the surface, her arms flailing and con-
sciousness seeking only one objective, something to
grab. Nothing else mattered now except the instinct of
survival. Her ears felt blocked and roaring, her head
bursting, and the sharp voice sounded a long way off.
Hands grasped at her, pushing her away, and she felt
herself go under again. The brute was going to leave
her to drown, and it was all his fault ...

'Do not struggle!' the voice cried. 'I do not want to
hit you!'

'Help me!' she gasped. 'I can't——'

He seemed to be going away. Faintly she heard the
exclamation: 'You will drown both of us!' before the
turbulent waters closed over her head, shutting out
everything except the roaring bursting pressure in her
head. Blackness swamped in, she was going down,
choking, and then suddenly she was trying to gasp in
blessed air. A bar was hard under her chin and sun
blinded into her eyes, making a glistening blur of the
sky. The bar was the wrist of the stranger, and he was
drawing her backwards through the heaving waves. A
great limpness pervaded her and all the fight went out
of her spirit. She closed her eyes weakly, some basic
instinct warning her to make no further struggle or the
consequences might be fatal ...

Her erstwhile pursuer towed her unresisting body
back towards the safety of the shore, one lean strong
hand hooked under her throat, keeping her mouth
above the invading surge of the sea, and the other
aiding the propulsion of his powerful leg strokes beneath her. When at last firm sand rose into shallows

he found his feet and scooped Laurel effortlessly into his
arms, to carry her a little way along the beach and then
lay her face down on a dark blue towelling robe. He
bent over her, his breathing only slightly quickened
from his exertions, and placed his hands down on her
back to apply pressure. But at their touch she gave a
violent shudder.

Dreadful realisation was already breaking through
her daze, and she tried to curl up, trying to hide herself,
even as coughing and retching overtook her with its
grim reaction to her dangerous experience.

He sat back on his heels, his dark face tautening with
anger, and snapped: 'You would prefer to recover un-
aided, it seems.'

Between the horrible spasms she choked, 'Go away—
you——'

'It is rather late for that, you foolish *niña*.' With a
scornful gesture he pulled free a wide fold of the robe
and dropped it across her nakedness. 'But then only a
woman would try to argue when her lungs are awash
with sea water.'

Laurel could not answer. She just wanted to die.

The next few minutes were the most distressing she
had ever endured in all her life. Nature's method of
trying to counteract the effects of being half drowned
was basic and very physical, and even Laurel's painful
awareness of the grim, silent presence nearby could not
stop her from being very sick. When at last she felt she
could draw breath freely through a rasped throat and
aching air passages she was too weak to do anything but
huddle miserably into the blue robe and knuckle the
tears out of sore, streaming eyes.

'So you begin to recover, *señorita*.'

The chill tones held a note of barely restrained anger,
but Laurel was beyond response other than the faintest
movement of her head. Her hair clung in matted
streaks round her face and dripped runnels of water
down her neck and shoulders, and her entire being
ached. She felt awful, and she wished with all her heart
that she was anywhere else in the world but this lonely

beach with its other, impossible occupant.

But it seemed he was not satisfied with her silence.

'Perhaps you feel recovered enough to explain your folly,' he suggested icily.

'Folly! Mine?' Laurel turned her head at last, stung into defence. 'But it was your fault! You started it! You——'

Her voice faltered and ebbed away as she encountered the sheer arrogant power of her adversary, face to face for the first time.

This was no slightly built Latin with melting eyes and warm mouth, who would woo a woman with velvet words and sinuous charm. This man had the proud head of a grandee, the arrogant, dominating eyes of a conquistador, the broad, corded steel torso of an athlete, the visage of a classical god, and the kind of magnetism beside which a lesser man would pale into insignificance. He was kneeling now, his brief scarlet swim trunks a splash of vivid colour that deepened the rich, dark gold tan of his body, but his height would undoubtedly be in the six foot region when he stood erect.

'Well,' he said, apparently wearying of her scrutiny, 'you were about to accuse me ... of what, señorita?'

'I was all right until you came, following me, refusing to let me swim in peace and——'

'Following you!' His dark eyes flashed. 'Why did you refuse to heed my warnings? We might both have drowned through your stupid, juvenile folly!'

Laurel stared at him as though he had taken leave of his senses. 'What warnings? How dare you accuse me, when all the time you were—were——'

'I was trying to prevent a trespasser from encountering the danger she seemed ignorant of, or oblivious to, but to which I am beginning to wish I had consigned her,' he interposed grimly. His mouth tightened as he stared at her unbelieving expression. 'Oh, yes, señorita, you were trespassing, and you were in very real danger.'

Laurel was beginning to feel very cold and shaky. But her spirit was returning and she said stubbornly, 'I met no danger until you arrived, señor.'

His dark brows went up. 'No? Perhaps you will remain silent until I convince you?' Without waiting for further argument he continued in the same icy tone: 'The *ensenada* looks idyllic, does it not? The sea calm and blue and inviting, the beach smooth and golden. Certainly one may bathe and swim here in perfect safety—provided one does not venture near *el vórtice*.'

El vórtice ... Vortex? Laurel started, and the stranger's mouth betrayed a cynical curve of amusement.

'I think perhaps you understand a trifle more of my language than you would admit. The translation you seek is indeed the whirlpool, and the word itself should be sufficient to strike fear into your heart, *señorita*.'

'There is a whirlpool out there?' she faltered.

He nodded. 'Near the base of the headland.'

She felt ice creep through her veins and she moved her head unbelievingly. 'I didn't know. I——'

'Yet you chose to ignore and defy my warnings, *señorita*.'

She licked dry lips. 'I didn't realise. I—I thought——' She stopped, unable to voice the truth, and again that scornful curve etched his mouth.

'You thought perhaps I pursued you for more blatant purpose, did you not?'

'What else was I to think?'

He inclined his head, and mocking lights entered his dark eyes. 'I assure you, *señorita*, I did not realise the reason for your strange folly—until it was almost too late. By then I had no alternative but to do what was necessary.' He paused. 'I have heard of the English girl's determination to flout all convention, but I did not expect to find one, *desnuda*, within my own boundaries. I must request that in future you show a token respect while a guest of this island, *señorita*. This is not the Riviera.'

A sudden thought of Yvonne flashed into Laurel's mind, bringing a wry twist to her mouth. She sighed. 'No, *señor*, I realise that. And if I'd known ...'

There was a world of bitterness left unspoken, but

more clearly conveyed than perhaps she realised.

He said smoothly, 'Then we shall consider the matter closed, *señorita*.'

But it wasn't as easy as that. By now Laurel wanted only to escape. She was remembering the sudden unexpected iciness of the water, no doubt the first indication of the dreaded vortex into which she had come so near to being drawn—but she would never have gone so far out but for this arrogant stranger's advent. She supposed she would have to thank him for bringing her out, give him the benefit of the doubt that he had indeed pursued her only to warn her ... She looked up at him.

'I—I know very little of your language—I didn't realise you were trying to warn me.'

'I said the matter was closed.' He was looking at her with a curious intensity, and Laurel felt colour come into her pale cheeks.

She said awkwardly, 'Well, thank you for—for saving my life.'

He raised one hand in a silencing gesture. 'You are feeling better now?'

She nodded. 'I—I have to get dressed ... my clothes...' She clutched the robe tight, and once again met that curious intensity of his regard. He showed no sign of making a polite retreat, and she felt fresh waves of resentment. 'Do I have to spell it out?' she hissed between taut lips.

'No, *señorita*.' He got lithely to his feet, and looking up at him she knew she had made no mistake in estimation of his stature. Towering above her and looking down at her small huddled form, he wore a sardonic smile. 'Again, it is a little late for feminine ... *pudor*, *señorita*.'

She did not recognise the word, but guessed instinctively that the English equivalent he sought was modesty and anger rose in her, making her scramble to her feet. 'It is certainly *not* too late as far as I am concerned, *señor*—oh!'

In her hasty attempt to rise, clutching the robe round

her and endeavouring to turn her back on him at the same time, she experienced a wave of giddiness and almost fell. Instantly she was caught and steadied by two hard hands.

She fought the trembling weakness, hating the moments of dependence on this man and the fact that despite it all her body tensed to the intimacy of his warm hard contact against herself through the single flimsy barrier between them.

'I think you are not recovered—the time of shock has set in,' he said sharply. 'Sit down, *señorita*, and tell me where you left your possessions. I will bring them to you.'

She could do little but obey, and a few moments later he returned, carrying the basket and the little bundle of clothing. 'And now,' he told her, 'I am going to swim. Please enrobe yourself, and feel assured that my attention will *not* be directed towards yourself, *señorita*.' He hesitated, looking down at her wan, drawn features, and that curious quirk touched his mouth again. 'Perhaps you will be better convinced if I say frankly that neither your present appearance nor your frame of mind is liable to inflame a man's desire—or even a temptation to play,' he paused, snapping impatient fingers for the expression he wanted then exclaiming triumphantly, 'peeping Tom!'

Before she could react to this calculated show of insolence he turned and took three long strides into the sea.

Laurel began to feel as though she had been badly winded. She watched the dark head and the feathering arms cleaving through deeper water, and then expelled a long breath of rage. How dared he! Of all the insufferable, arrogant, infuriating males she'd ever met this one took the palm!

With savage movements she pulled on her clothes and tried to comb her hair into a semblance of tidiness. By the time she had finished her anger was spent and self-pity replaced it. No doubt she looked a mess, but if he'd been half drowned and forced to submit to the high-handed treatment of an arrogant brute like himself he wouldn't be looking or feeling exactly like the Hallelujah Chorus. And if he hadn't come barging in on her in the first place it would never have happened. She'd have finished her cooling dip, dressed and dried off in the sun and been away without any bother. Laurel put on her shoes, shook the robe free of sand and folded it up, and with a grimace of distaste scooped sand over the horrid traces of her misfortune. There, that was everything. With luck she would be gone before he returned.

She looked across the gilt-dappled waves, and saw that he was still swimming a little farther along. Good, that saved any argument. Laurel picked up her basket and turned to make her way back the way she had come. The thought of the long, long walk was daunting, but to stay and rest here was even more so. She had covered only a dozen yards before the peremptory voice sounded.

He was emerging from the water at a point a little way ahead. Within moments he had barred her path.

'Where are you going, *señorita*?'

'Back to the guest house, of course.'

'The Allens' *pensión*? Do you think that is wise, *señorita*? It is all of ten *kilómetros* distant.'

'So what?' She faced him wearily. 'What do you suggest? That I camp on the beach? *Trespassing*?'

'I would suggest nothing of the sort. We are within ten minutes' walk of my home. There you may shower and refresh yourself. Come, *señorita*, this way.'

He stood there, tall and dominant, glints of impatience narrowing his dark eyes, and Laurel took a step back, shaking her head.

'No, thank you, *señor*,' she said coldly. 'I appreciate your offer, but no.'

'Why not?' He looked amazed, as though no one had ever contradicted him quite so flatly and the experience was not to his liking at all.

'Because I don't want to,' she said quietly, turning away. 'Goodbye, *señor*.'

'*Un minuto!*'

Suddenly her wrist was seized and she was swung round to face blazing eyes.

'You foolish *señorita*! Why are you afraid of me?'

'Let go of me! I'm not afraid of you!'

'Then why do you abuse my offer of hospitality?'

Laurel tore herself free. 'I think that should be fairly obvious, *señor*! First you almost cause me to drown, then you accuse me of trespassing—and then you try to make fun of me! Do you wonder I abuse your hospitality?'

For a moment he looked as though he might strike her, then control tightened his lean jaw muscles and set his mouth into a long taut line. 'You do not know what you say, *señorita*. I shall ignore your ill-founded accusations and suggest that you are in no fit state to make the journey back to your *pensión*.'

'Fit or not, I'm going to make it. Nothing would induce me to stay here a moment longer,' Laurel blazed at him. 'Can't you take no for an answer? Can't you understand that all I want is to get away from this place and forget the most—the most embarrassing experience I've ever had? No, *señor*, I do not want your hospitality, nor do I ever want to see *you* again!'

She turned then, tears of anger and weakness smarting her eyes, and began to run. Twice she stumbled, but each time fear of him and further humiliation kept her hurrying desperately to where the steep rough track led up to the path through the groves. Only when she reached the lengthening shadows of the trees did she allow herself to pause and glance over her shoulder.

He was still there.

But in that moment as she turned he also moved, slinging the blue robe carelessly across his broad shoulder and striding away towards the opposite end of the bay. His shadow lay long on the sand, sharp black against the deepening golden tones of the waning afternoon, and something made Laurel put a hand to her thumping heart.

Although no chill breeze had sprung up to temper

the heat she was shivering and her skin had turned clammy with perspiration. The arrogant stranger was out of sight now, but for some reason Laurel could not forget that long black shadow on the sand.

It was almost as disturbing as its owner.

CHAPTER THREE

LAUREL was exhausted by the time she got back to the
guest house. Her unnerving experience of that afternoon had taken its toll, and despite her having stopped
three times to rest during the return journey her legs
trembled as she entered the gate, telling her they would
not have carried her much farther.

It was dark too, and she had been thankful to see the
warm golden radiance of the lovely old Spanish
wrought iron lanterns beckoning her back to rest and
security. There was no sign of Yvonne, and the lamp-
lit terrace was deserted as Laurel went wearily along it
to return her basket. All she wanted was to ease her
aching limbs into a warm bath and then seek her bed,
which she fully intended to do immediately after the
evening meal. Fortunately Mr and Mrs Allen kept to
more traditional English mealtimes and dinner was at
eight in the evenings—rather earlier than was the
custom in Spanish society. She left the basket outside
the door that led to the kitchen quarters, and was crossing the wide hall towards the stairs when someone
called: 'Miss Daneway!'

It was Mrs Allen, wife of the proprietor.

Reluctantly Laurel stopped, but Mrs Allen did not
come towards her. Instead the older woman inclined
her head towards her private sitting room. 'If you can
spare a few moments,' she said in a low voice, 'I would
like a few words with you, Miss Daneway.'

'Yes, of course.' Making an effort to hide her weariness, Laurel went into the small, simply furnished room
that faced the rear of the villa. The thought flashed
into her mind that something had happened to Yvonne
during her own absence—and alarm came into her eyes.
'Is something wrong?' she asked urgently.

Mrs Allen shook her head instantly, but there was a

faintly disquieting look about her that did nothing to
banish Laurel's alarm.

'Please sit down.' Mrs Allen indicated a chair and
then sat down herself. 'I hope you won't be offended
by what I'm going to say—as a rule I never interfere
in the affairs of our guests, but I'm rather worried.'

'But why?' Laurel's hands tightened on the arms of
the chair. A wild fear rose that somehow word of her
experience had already percolated to the guest house
—oh, why hadn't she kept her mouth shut about where
she was staying?—and a complaint had been made.
'What happened—what have I done?' she whispered.

'Oh, it isn't you, my dear!' Mrs Allen smiled. 'If all
our guests were as little bother as yourself we'd be on
velvet. Unfortunately, they're not. No, it's Miss Searle,
I'm afraid.'

Yvonne! Inwardly Laurel groaned. What had her
spoiled young charge done now?

'I know she's very young, and she's obviously used
to getting her own way,' Mrs Allen went on with a note
of apology in her tone, 'but for her own sake one of us
must warn her.'

'About what?'

'About making a silly little idiot of herself over one
of my waiters.' Mrs Allen's lips tightened. 'Were you
aware of this—this flirtation in which she's getting involved with Renaldo?'

'Oh no!' Dismay clouded Laurel's face. 'I had no
idea—we've only been here three days. Today is the
first time I've left her on her own.'

'Well, she didn't waste the opportunity,' said Mrs
Allen, grimly. 'I caught them in the garden—oh, just
innocent skylarking, don't worry about that—but I
believe they'd spent the afternoon on the beach.' Mrs
Allen's expression softened. 'You see, my dear, trouble
starts so easily. Renaldo is young and attractive, and
knows it, but young Spanish girls of good family just
don't flaunt themselves in the way our girls do. Oh,
dear,' she sighed, 'I'm not putting this very clearly, am
I? You see, the island has never become a popular

tourist spot—the Patrón would never allow it to go that way—and consequently life still tends to go on much the same as it has done for centuries, especially with being so far from mainland Spain.'

Laurel looked slightly puzzled and wished Mrs Allen would get on with it; she felt so desperately tired.

Mrs Allen, mistaking the puzzled look, smiled. 'Oh, yes, Destino is a Spanish possession, has been for about four hundred years, but the true ruler of Destino is the Conde—you must have noticed the *castillo* up on the headland—and he permits change of only the more ethical social progress. We have a small but very up-to-date hospital, a new school, and no one is allowed to know poverty, but otherwise . . .'

Mrs Allen's shrug was expressive, and Laurel made a weary murmur of acknowledgement.

'So that's why I must ask you to speak to Miss Searle. Try to explain to her that what to the average English teenager is merely fun and flirtation is wanton behaviour in the opinion of the locals. To them a girl is cheapening herself if she encourages a man to flirt with her. Of course the young men think it's wonderful, naturally, especially those like Renaldo and his brother who have worked seasons on the Costa Brava, and came home boasting about their conquests and the presents women showered on them. It's pathetic, really, when women are as lonely as that, but we don't want anything like that happening here—the dust has hardly settled after the Lang business.'

Laurel suppressed a sigh. Plainly her hostess was wound up for the evening now. More from politeness than curiosity she asked, 'What was that?'

'A family we had staying here a while ago. They had a daughter, a pretty child, terribly repressed and cosseted, probably with her being an only child who was born to them when they were almost into middle age. She'd never met anyone like Renaldo in her sheltered existence and she went crazy over him. You see,' Mrs Allen lowered her voice confidingly, 'Mrs Lang had been ill and Mr Lang brought them here so that she

could recuperate. He stayed for a week to see them
settled in, then went back to his business, planning to
return in the spring to take them home again, when the
worst of the English winter would be over. But by then
it was too late for poor Sara!'

'But why?' At last Laurel was jerked back to attention by a dark note of meaning in Mrs Allen's tone.
'What happened?'

'She was pregnant.'

Laurel exclaimed aloud. 'And you mean it ... happened here?'

Mrs Allen nodded. 'Yes. And Renaldo was responsible. He admitted it—said she'd tempted him. Poor
Sara Lang! She scarcely knew the meaning of the word.
Oh, he offered to marry her, prompted by authority, but
Mr Lang said he wasn't going to have his only daughter
pitched into a shotgun wedding at her age. She was
only sixteen. And I doubt if the truth would have
come out when it did if we hadn't happened to have
a retired nurse staying here at the time. She didn't take
long to realise why Sara was so white and scared and
sick in the mornings. I'll never forget that day when she
said straight out: "That girl's pregnant." And of course
the balloon went up. Mr Lang had just arrived the day
before, so pleased because his wife looked so well,
and then a shock like that ... Anyway, he hustled them
back home—I suppose he wanted to see if an abortion
was possible—and the Conde was furious. I've often
wondered what happened to Sara ...'

At last Mrs Allen dried up, and Laurel felt a sick
pang of unease. No wonder the woman was concerned
about Yvonne, if the silly girl had started fooling
around with the island's Casanova—except that the real
Casanova had been reputed to take care that his amours
did not suffer from his carelessness, Laurel reflected a
trifle hysterically. Heavens, and Yvonne's father had
sent her here to get her away from danger!

She stood up. 'Thank you for warning me, Mrs Allen.
I'll certainly speak to Yvonne.' Not that Yvonne would
take much notice, she thought resignedly.

'Have you had a nice day?' Mrs Allen asked, with a bright changing-the-subject smile.

Laurel made the obvious and totally untruthful response, and escaped at last. She'd had her bath, there wouldn't be time now, she thought with a flash of resentment. A quick shower before she changed for dinner would be all she'd have time for. With a sigh, she went in search of Yvonne, determined to get the unpleasant business done with. Although Yvonne was probably a different proposition altogether from the unfortunate Sara Lang. Yvonne was fully aware of the more basic facts of life, if not the subtler ones.

But Yvonne was not to be found. Laurel searched the gardens and then gave it up, somewhat reassured by a glimpse of Renaldo in the dining room as she passed the open door. She would talk to Yvonne to-night.

But she was somewhat surprised by Yvonne's pale face when they met in the dining room. The younger girl did not come in until almost all the guests were at the tables, and she was decidedly subdued. To Laurel's enquiry, however, she merely shrugged, offering no explanation, and proceeded to toy with curried chicken and rice. She did not eat much, and left half of her iced lime cream, then refused coffee. Laurel watched her sink a despondent chin into one hand, then leaned forward.

'Yvonne, what's the matter? You've hardly eaten anything.'

'I don't want any more.'

'But why not? Is something wrong?'

Yvonne sat up petulantly, giving an impatient sigh. 'I feel sick. If you must know, I've started the curse and I've a lousy headache. Now leave me alone. I'm going to bed.'

She stood up, almost overturning her coffee cup, and flounced out of the room. Several heads turned to watch her exit, the Colonel's wife stiff with disapproval, and one or two glanced back to Laurel with something like sympathy in their expressions.

Laurel finished her coffee and did not linger afterwards or join the other guests on the terrace, which seemed to be a customary place of adjournment after the evening meal, where some of the guests partook of their coffee and others had drinks. She went straight up to the big, airy bedroom she and Yvonne shared, entering quietly, with the intention of offering aspirins or whatever comfort she could to Yvonne.

The room was in darkness, except for the little lamp at the side of Yvonne's bed, and the slight figure of Yvonne herself was curled up beneath the coverlet. Laurel went to the bedside.

'Is there anything I can get you?' she said softly.

There was no response. Yvonne's face was buried in the pillow, and her dark hair was spread in a tumbled cloud on the snowy linen. She was sound asleep.

Laurel straightened. Better not wake her; a sound sleep would probably see her right by the morning. It was still early, not yet ten o'clock, and Laurel wavered; it seemed ridiculously early to turn in, but she was very tired, even though her shower and the food had restored her to a certain extent.

She went to the window, drawing aside the flax curtains and looking out into the night. There was a small balcony, in the traditional lacework of black wrought iron with hanging baskets of geraniums and lobelia, and blue painted shutters that could be closed against the fierce storms that could sweep in from the Atlantic when the weather was in less benign mood. In daytime the balcony afforded a glorious, picture-postcard view of the sea and bay; now, under a thin crescent moon, it took on an air of mystery. The lanterns in the garden cast pools of amber amid the black shadowy shapes of trees and shrubs and the lovely old ornamental urns and statuary with which the grounds were dotted, and the night insects fluttered palely, the sound of the cicadas a soft background music to their flight.

It was a wildly romantic setting, and for a moment it evoked strange echoes that dispelled Laurel's present worries. If only Phil could have been here ... if they could forget that miserable night and start again ... if, after all, she could only discover that she had been completely mistaken, that he was sincere in all he said, she would say she was sorry with all her heart ... Perhaps when she got home it might not be too late ...

She closed her eyes, seeking Phil's face in her mental view, and suddenly she was trembling. Although Phil was in her mind the picture she saw was not of him ... Almost angrily she turned back to the shadowy room. It was bad enough that a stranger should invade her innocent privacy, cause her to half drown and endanger her life, without prevading her thoughts with his image ...

Forcing her mind to concentrate on the minutiae of undressing and brushing her teeth, winding her watch, tidying the things Yvonne had left strewn about the room, and finally giving a sigh of gratitude for the blissful coolness between the sheets, Laurel prepared for sleep. But the dark and quiet seemed to welcome her unwelcome adversary. In slow motion he recreated the entire sequence, his voice, the burnishing sun and the crystal waves, his arms and his thick black hair, his mockery and his anger, his arrogance and his sheer compelling power ...

Laurel turned and tossed in her efforts to escape. Her body began to burn with the effects of hot sun and salt water—and the re-awakening knowledge of an unknown man's arms holding it at his mercy. Had he ... looked at her ...?

If only she had resisted that crazy impulse to swim!

She curled up into a small huddled shape under the clothes, as though the subconscious action would exorcise the memory of those moments of total vulnerability. She didn't even know who he was ...

But there was a strange kind of relief in this knowledge. Fate willing, she would never cross his path again. The humiliation of a second meeting would be unbearable.

At last she succumbed to sheer weariness, drifting into an uneasy sleep. The soft secret rustles of the night receded beyond her hearing as her breathing steadied, and the new, stealthy sounds which began some twenty minutes later did not intrude into her slumber.

Yvonne gave a sigh of impatience and slid cautiously from under the coverlet, giving frequent glances towards the other bed as she began to dress. Her face was pale and anxious, and a hint of fear was in her eyes when she strained to see the time by her small jewelled wristwatch. Impatience made her careless as she picked up her sandals and tiptoed towards the door. A buckle on one of the slingbacks was loose and as she opened the door inch by inch the strap gave way and the sandal clattered down on the polished wood surround beyond the big Spanish rugs that were scattered on the floor.

Laurel stirred, and gave a murmur.

There was a stifled imprecation, a swift blur of movement, and then the door closed.

Suddenly Laurel was wide awake. She sat up, groping for the lamp switch and blinking in the flare of brilliance. Then her dazzled eyes took in the empty bed opposite, and with a cry of alarm she sprang out of bed and ran to the door. Yvonne had reached the head of the staircase.

Laurel sped towards her. 'What's the matter? Are you ill?'

Yvonne made a gesture to ward off interference. 'No —go back to bed.'

'But why are—where are you going?'

'Shut up!' Yvonne's mouth grimaced angrily. 'Do you want to wake the place?' she hissed. 'I'm just going downstairs.'

'But what for?' Laurel was still more puzzled than angry at the younger girl's rudeness. 'Why didn't you wake me? I'd have got whatever you——'

'I did wake you—worse luck!' Yvonne began to descend the wide carved oak staircase, her bare feet noiseless on the carpet pads.

'Yes, but——' Laurel gave a hunted look round at the still closed doors along the galleried landing, and began to follow. 'Yvonne, why are you fully dressed? What's——'

'Because I'm going out. And don't try to stop me!'

'But you're not—not without an explanation.' Laurel shot out a restraining hand. She caught Yvonne's wrist. 'Now what's going on?'

'I told you—nothing!' Yvonne tried to tug free as some instinct made Laurel hold tight to the slender wrist. Then a door opened and a portly dressing-gowned figure peered out.

'Is something wrong?' Mr Binkley looked for the source of the disturbance, then changed his tone from curiosity to archness. 'Ah, our young friends. Is this a secret assignation, ladies?'

'Oh, damn!' Yvonne spun round and began to run back up the stairs and along to her room, passing the somewhat astonished Mr Binkley and leaving him staring after her. The door slammed, and after a brief hesitation Laurel also turned back, brushing past Mr Binkley without speaking; at least Yvonne was clothed, which was more than she could say of herself, Laurel thought bitterly. It just hadn't been her day!

Her face was flaming as she entered the bedroom and grabbed her wrap, and by now she was in no mood for excuses. Yvonne had hurled herself on to the bed and was weeping noisily, but Laurel said sharply: 'Now what was all that about?'

'It's all your fault! You've ruined everything.' Yvonne wriggled furiously and squirmed her face into the pillow. 'Oh, go away—I hate you!'

'What the devil do you mean?' Laurel was fast losing patience. 'You were supposed to be feeling off-colour, then you try to sneak out. Why?'

There was no response, and Laurel crossed to the bedside. 'Where were you going?'

'To meet somebody, if you must know!'

'Meet somebody? At this time of night?'

'And now it's too late, and I'll never get it back. Oh, what am I going to do?'

Yvonne burst into a fresh spate of weeping, and Laurel stared down at her with puzzled eyes. What on earth was the girl talking about? A conviction that something was wrong, much more than some teenage escapade, began to supersede Laurel's anger, and she bent to touch Yvonne's shoulder.

'I don't understand. What's too late? What is it you'll never get back? I think you'd better tell me, Yvonne,' she said quietly.

'It's my ring.'

'What ring?'

Yvonne sniffed miserably. 'My ruby ring—the snaky one. It's gold and the eye is a real ruby. Daddy gave it to me for my birthday—it cost a bomb. He'll be furious.'

'You've lost it?'

Yvonne nodded, trying to find a dry corner of the soaked little tissue balled in her hand. 'Today.'

Laurel gave an exclamation of concern. She remembered the ring very well; Yvonne had worn it that day her father had taken the two girls out to lunch, and its strange Eastern opulence had instantly caught Laurel's attention, although she had not made any comment on its fascination. It was obviously gold, beautifully engraved and inlaid with fine silvery wire patterns, and the glowing red eye of the head had seemed almost alive. No wonder, if it was a precious ruby. But what on earth had possessed Yvonne to bring such a valuable item of jewellery with her? Laurel reached for a clean tissue from the box on the dressing table and pushed it into Yvonne's hand.

'When did you last see it?'

Yvonne buried her face in the tissue. 'I'm not sure.'

'Did you wear it today?'

There was a pause, then a muffled sound that Laurel took to be assent. Suppressing a sigh, Laurel persisted: 'Well, where did you go while I was out?'

'Nowhere in particular. Just the beach.' Abruptly Yvonne sat up, and now her tears had vanished, leaving her face sulky. 'Oh, what's the good? I'll just have to say I lost it, won't I?'

But she avoided Laurel's eyes, and Laurel felt a rush of suspicion. Yvonne was hiding something.

Laurel said sharply, 'Stop lying to me. You said it was too late before. What did you mean by that? And why were you trying to sneak out?' There was a pause, and Laurel added in the same sharp tone, 'If that ring doesn't turn up I'll have to report the loss to Mrs Allen, you know, and she'll have to inform the police.'

'Oh no!' Yvonne looked up with such horror on her face that Laurel was shocked. 'No, you mustn't say anything! Promise!'

A flash of perception made Laurel subdue her impatience. Beneath the outward display of teenage tears and rebellion Yvonne was frightened. Laurel sat down on the bed and touched Yvonne's arm. 'What is it?' she asked gently. 'Can't you tell me?'

Yvonne turned away. 'Only if you promise not to interfere and tell anybody.'

It was stalemate. Laurel sighed. 'I only want to help you.'

'Then help me by not making a fuss—let me get out of here without waking all the old pussies.'

Laurel lost patience again. 'Listen, I wasn't born yesterday. Who are you planning to meet? I don't believe you've lost that ring—it's just an excuse.'

'All right!' Yvonne flung round. 'I'm going to meet Renaldo—he's got my ring!'

'Oh no!' Laurel paled. 'But why? And——'

'We were on the beach this afternoon, swimming and fooling around. I forgot I was wearing the ring, until he noticed it, and said I might lose it in the water.' Yvonne's mouth trembled. 'I was going to run back here and put it away, but he said he would look after it for me, on the gold chain he wears round his neck.'

Laurel nodded grimly. She remembered seeing Renaldo during the day, out of his waiter's livery and in more informal jeans with a cotton shirt open to the waist, revealing the long gold chain and a gilt medallion that glinted against his olive skin.

'So he threaded it on the chain,' Yvonne went on, 'but afterwards, when it was time to come back, and I asked him for it, he said I had to take it myself. We were laughing, and he caught me and started to kiss me, and——'

Laurel's mouth tightened. The age-old moral blackmail was inevitable in such circumstances. 'And he refused to return it.'

Yvonne nodded. 'He said he'd give it back to me tonight, in the cove at midnight.'

'You little simpleton!' Laurel groaned. 'Do you really believe he'll return it? Can't you see it's just his way of fun at your expense?'

Yvonne gave a choked laugh. 'I thought you were going to say he would have his way with me! Don't worry, I know what I'm doing, and I can deal with Renaldo.'

'Famous last words. You haven't been very successful so far,' Laurel reminded her. 'For goodness' sake, grow up. Renaldo's been boasting about his conquests —and the presents they buy him. Mrs Allen told me.'

'And Renaldo told me himself,' Yvonne said triumphantly. 'He told me everything. How sometimes girls on holiday are lonely, and he feels sorry for them, and his job means he has to be friendly to them. But he isn't like that, not the way you're implying. As though he were a common beach lizard.'

'I think you've said it yourself,' Laurel told her flatly, abandoning all pretence of sternness, 'and I think you know that you're heading for hurt and disillusion.' She sighed and stood up. 'I'll get your ring back for you.'

'You!'

'Yes.' Laurel was stripping off her night robe. 'I promised your father I would look after you, and I mean to do just that. I'll get that ring, even if I have to rouse the local *guardia*.'

'No!' Yvonne grabbed her arm. 'Not the police— you promised! He'll deny it! Don't you see—it's only my word against his. He'll say I lost it, and I'll never see it again.' She sank down on the bed and her slight shoulders trembled with renewed sobs.

'You will,' said Laurel, with an assurance she was far from feeling. 'Now get back into bed—and stay there. Or I *will* raise a fuss.'

Yvonne subsided without further argument, and a moment or so later Laurel went quietly downstairs and let herself out of the silent guest house. She was too angry to feel nervous, but as she hurried down the narrow winding track to the village she began to wish the island were just a little more tourist-orientated. Although people were still abroad and from the open windows behind the little iron balconies came lamp-light and voices, occasionally the crying of a baby and often the blare of radios, it seemed to close her out and heighten the sense of loneliness. An English voice and her own tongue would have been comforting, and when the soft fur of a cat brushed her legs before it vanished into the shadowy courtyard of the inn she could not restrain a small gasp of shock.

Then she came out of the last narrow street and saw the open countryside stretching away into the night. A few minutes' walk would bring her to the beach and the cove which was the trysting place. Her anger had now dissipated, leaving edgy tremors playing down her spine. What if Renaldo refused to hand over the ring? She could scarcely take it from him by force. For the first time Laurel began to realise she was as foolish as Yvonne. Renaldo might not even be waiting. He might be intending to play along for the rest of the holiday, alternately teasing and promising, then withholding. But she must go on now, Laurel decided reluctantly.

To her relief the moon was rising, casting a silvery radiance over the path that led down the rocky incline to the beach. The rocks and foliage cast inky shadows, and the sea made its soft, lonely music, unbroken by the birds' calls and the sounds of the day. Laurel stepped down on to the soft shifting sand and looked around her. She could see no one, nor hear any indication that anyone but herself was about at this eerie hour of midnight. Stifling the impulse to turn back, she walked along the beach for a short distance, then stood still, anger returning with the thought that she had come on a wild goose chase. Today had certainly brought its measure of trouble to herself and Yvonne—and from similar sources, she thought ironically. So much for the local Latin Lotharios! In future she would take good care not to——

'Señorita?'

A small cry of shock rose in Laurel's throat. She spun round to seek the presence of her adversary, and for a moment could see no one. Then a shadow moved at the base of the cliff and a chuckle stole from the darkness.

'So you come at last, señorita. I was beginning to think you were going to disappoint me.'

He seemed to expect her to go to him, towards the great gaping fissure of what looked like a cave or deep indentation on the rock face. Laurel remained still, obeying an instinct to stay silent. Presently the dark shadow moved and Renaldo swaggered into the thin silver swathe of moonlight. She could see the glint of his teeth and suddenly she realised that her own face was in shadow, and he had not yet realised her identity.

She said coldly, 'I'm afraid you *are* going to be disappointed, *señor*.'

He started, recognition dawning, and the smile disappeared. 'I do not understand. Where is the Señorita Searle?'

'At the hotel.'

'What are you doing here?' he demanded, moving closer to stare at her with snapping black eyes. 'Why does she not keep her appointment?'

'That doesn't concern you. Where is her ring?'

'What ring?' He pretended puzzlement. 'I do not know what you mean.'

'I think you know very well.' Laurel gripped the edges of her jacket with fingers that wanted to tremble. 'The ring that belongs to Señorita Searle, which you did not return to her this afternoon.' Suddenly she caught the glint of brightness on his little finger as he moved. 'You are wearing it, I think, at this very moment.'

He moved the hand behind his back. 'You are not the owner, *señorita*. I promised to return the ring to its owner, and no one else.'

'You had no right to take it in the first place!'

'Are you threatening me, *señorita*?' His voice held a note of veiled menace.

Laurel stood her ground. 'Not yet. I am demanding the return of my friend's property.'

'I do not like demands of that kind, *señorita*. Why do you not ask me nicely? It was only a little joke.'

'My sense of humour never learned Spanish.' Laurel took a deep breath. 'The joke is over, Renaldo. It's very late, and I'm very tired. Now give me that ring.'

He stepped back a pace, his dark eyes looking her up and down. 'In a moment. You are making me angry, *señorita*, and I think you have deliberately stolen something from me.'

Laurel lost patience. 'For heaven's sake, stop being so ridiculous! What could I possibly have stolen from you?'

'You have robbed me of the moments I have looked forward to all evening—my meeting with the enchanting Señorita Yvonne. Oh yes,' he moved again, close to her, 'she has told me of you, of the authority her father gives to you, of the yoke you put on her freedom.'

This carried a ring of truth that was undeniable. She could almost hear the wilful Yvonne uttering the words. Laurel suppressed a sigh of despair and a natural impulse to defend herself. She said coldly, 'I'm not going to argue with you. Now are you going to hand over that ring, or do I go to the *guardia*?'

'So!' his breath came in a warm hiss against her cheek, 'you do threaten me! Or perhaps I am mistaken!' Suddenly his hands shot out and caught her by the shoulders. 'Perhaps you have another reason, *señorita*.'

'Another reason?' Laurel started back. 'Whatever do you mean?'

His hands tightened, forestalling her move and maintaining their imprisoning grip. The moonlight caught the shadows in his unpleasant smile as he put his face close to stare into her frightened eyes. 'I mean,' he taunted, 'that you are curious about me, *señorita*. Perhaps even envious of your friend.'

'Envious! Of—— Why, you conceited——!' Laurel almost stuttered with shock and disgust. Did he really imagine that was her true motive for keeping the appointment? She struggled angrily. 'I never heard such a stupid idea! Let me go! You must be——'

'Oh no!' Deftly he recaptured her, his slim, wiry fingers biting into the softness of her upper arms. 'They all say that—at first. So tell me, *señorita*, is your friend scared? Does she truly send you to pay her forfeit?'

'Forfeit! I'm paying no forfeit! Let me go—or I'll scream the beach down until——'

'No one will hear, silly English miss!' With a triumphant laugh he dragged her close and tried to kiss her desperately evading mouth. Her struggles only made him redouble his efforts, and Laurel realised that though he was slimly built and only an inch or so superior in height to herself his strength was steely and his determination no less so. Her thin jacket was being twisted round, its material straining and adding to her plight, and real fear came into her eyes as Renaldo gave an adroit jerk that pinned her right arm behind her back.

'Did you think you would cheat me?' he exclaimed hotly, fastening cruel fingers round her throat and forcing her to face him. 'Or perhaps you prefer to pretend at first!'

He laughed again, then Laurel's head was forced back under the onslaught of his mouth, her cry of desperation stifled as pain shot through her pinioned arm. Then suddenly the constricting jacket gave way and Renaldo's exploring hand roamed greedily over her breasts.

'*No!*' Laurel strained back frantically, kicking out wildly, and an oath escaped him.

'You little vixen, you will regret this!' Remorselessly he forced her down to the sand, and Laurel sobbed aloud as she fought for freedom. Fear coursed through her with the realisation of her plight. The ring was forgotten; all that mattered was escape—before Renaldo went completely berserk and raped her! There was a drumming in her ears, thudding above her gasping breaths and the writhing movements of Renaldo as he sought to pin her down on the shifting sand. With a desperate thrust she freed her arm and struck out wildly, and screamed an anguished: '*Help! Help!*' at the highest pitch of her voice.

The drumming stopped, there was a great shadow above, and then suddenly the dark shape and weight of Renaldo swung away and she saw the star-peppered sky above. There was a grunt and a cry, then a thud, and unbelievably she was free.

She rolled over and saw the great shadow, and thought she must be in a nightmare, and then hands were supporting her shoulders.

'*Señorita*, are you all right?'

The sharp question came from a long way through her daze. It couldn't be! Not rescue, and not a huge stallion pawing the sand only inches from her head— a great coal black, glistening brute. She must be dreaming it all. But the strong hands drawing her up to a sitting position were real, as was the dark head bending over her, and the voice that seemed strangely familiar.

She raised a hand to her brow, pushing back her disordered hair, and took a deep shuddering breath. The mists were clearing, and she was dimly aware of the other form tumbled on the sand a little distance away. Even as she moved she saw the spreadeagled figure of Renaldo stir and slowly pick himself up, then back away. Laurel found her voice.

'Stop him—he's got my ring!'

She made an effort to stand. After all she had gone

through she wasn't going to let him escape with the cause of all the trouble. Her rescuer took two strides away and shot out an arresting arm, while Laurel's legs buckled under her and she sank back on to the sand.

'What is this?' the tall stranger demanded. 'Have you robbed the *señorita* as well as attacking her?'

She heard Renaldo mumble something, and then a torrent of Spanish was exchanged. Moments later the stranger turned back, holding out an open palm, and the slim figure of Renaldo began to slink away into the darkness under the lee of the cliff.

'Is this your property?'

Laurel looked numbly at the ring lying on his outstretched palm and nodded, making no attempt to take it. 'At least, it belongs to my friend.'

'Perhaps you had better explain—and assure me that you are indeed unmolested.'

She knew now the identity of her rescuer—if not his name—and shame was covering her in a hot tide. 'I'm all right, thank you—but if you hadn't come ...' She tried to steady her voice, to stand up again, to straighten her dishevelled clothing, and found that none of her faculties would obey the dictates of her brain. Tears began to pour down her cheeks and her body to shake all over.

The stranger stood for a moment, looking down at her from his great height, then abruptly he stooped, and before she could protest he scooped her up into his arms as though she were a child.

'You do not seem all right,' he observed coolly. 'Twice in one day—do you make a habit of this?'

She shook her head, too spent to frame a coherent reply, and he turned to the black stallion, murmuring a soft command. Instantly its restive movements ceased. He said to Laurel, 'If I lift you so, can you mount and hold on until I do?'

She murmured a shaky assent, and felt herself lifted high and swung across the saddle. The world tipped dizzily, she grabbed at the smooth glossy neck, and then her rescuer was astride behind her, a firm arm grasping her waist and tilting her back against him.

'Relax and lean back,' instructed the deep voice, 'and draw up your knees a little—you will find the ride more comfortable.'

'It—it's very kind of you, *señor*,' she whispered as she obeyed, 'but you don't need to take me back. I could——'

'Return on foot? I do not think you are in a fit state to do that. Now please do not talk,' he instructed.

She felt the supreme power of the great black horse ripple beneath her as it moved off, and instinctively she braced herself against falling.

'I said *relax*,' came the quiet command. 'I will not allow you to fall.'

The terrifying gallop she had expected did not happen. As though it knew, or responded to its master's signal, the stallion moved smoothly along the beach at a sedate pace, yet seemingly unconscious of the double burden it carried. Gradually the trembling stilled in Laurel's body, and she began to relax in this strangely unexpected sense of security. It was not until a little while later that she realised they had passed the path from the beach which she should have taken to return through the village and hence to the guest house. She stirred wildly, and the hard arm round her waist tightened.

'Curb that alarm, *señorita*. I am taking you to my home—you are scarcely in a fit state to present yourself at the guest house.'

'But I——'

'Please allow me to know what is best for you. I am beginning to suspect you are incapable of knowing that for yourself. Surely you should not need my assurances that I and my household are perfectly civilised— you will come to far less harm than had I not happened on you tonight, while you were at the mercy of that insolent young pup.'

'Yes, *señor*, you are very kind, and I'm grateful. But it is after midnight.'

'So what?'

How did one answer that? Unwillingly Laurel subsided. There was much truth in what he said; had he not chanced to ride along the beach at that late hour the outcome to herself could have been shameful, if not tragic.

The strange sense of security returned to lull her into an acquiescence where she ceased to wonder where they were going or why he had been riding on the beach at midnight, and the gentle rise and fall of motion gradually carried her into a dreamlike kind of trance. The moonlight glimmered on the eternal wash of the sea, and the dark island might have been uninhabited apart from herself and the silent man whose warm strength against her back had become so utterly disarming. What did it matter? What did anything matter, except that her frightening experience was already receding into the limbo of a nightmare now gone.

The beach petered out a mile ahead, and under the lee of the headland a path wound steeply up the incline. The sandy scrub of the foreshore gave way to dense undergrowth and stunted trees, and then the path opened out into broad track. There was the scent of night blossoms unseen, and the secret stirrings of small nocturnal creatures to hint that life did abound after all. A sharp and raucous cry shrilled without warning, and a wild flurry disturbed the black, rustling leaves. Some bird, startled into wakefulness by their approach, Laurel decided, tensing, and then sighing as the echoes subsided. But the sound had been enough to wrench her back to reality.

She stared ahead, at the broad trellis of scrolled iron silhouetted like an arch of dark lace against the moonlit sky, the broad entrance through which they were already entering, and she saw the great outline glimmering beyond, the outline of towers, massive walls, and turreted stone previously glimpsed only from afar.

The shock of credulity coursed through her as she

recognised her destination. And an even greater shock of prescience brought a gasp to her lips. How had she failed to guess?

They had come to the *castillo*. And the dark stranger, who had dismounted, who was reaching up to lift her from the magnificent black stallion, and whose mocking smile glinted down at her while his arms held her steady, could be none other than . . . the Conde himself!

CHAPTER FOUR

'WELCOME to Valderosa!'

To the echoes of the mocking exclamation Laurel walked under the great stone arch that led into the castle. The hall within was high and cavernous, heavy with baroque carving and age-darkened paintings within plaster-gilt frames, and a huge old tapestry that covered almost one wall. There was a broad staircase with a gallery in the sombre shadows above, enough exquisitely carved old chests, high-backed chairs and baronial tables holding porcelain and precious metal curios to delight the heart of any antique lover, and high overhead a magnificent panelled and ornamented ceiling of rich cedarwood. The whole was lit by scrolled iron brackets set above the series of deep niches indenting the walls, and the warm amber radiance seemed to heighten the dreamlike state in which Laurel moved.

She turned, still dazed from the realisation of the true identity of her host, and gave a start of shock as she encountered the impersonal gaze of a stranger. A manservant in black had materialised silently from a side door and now looked beyond her to the tall figure of the Conde.

The Conde issued several rapid instructions, then turned to Laurel. 'Go with José. I will join you in a few moments, *señorita*.'

She guessed that he wished to stable his horse, and two thoughts conflicted in her mind; that he had little consideration for his servants when he would keep them up to wait on him until an hour as late as this, yet he was concerned enough to insist on offering hospitality to a stranger regardless of the time of day —or night.

The manservant betrayed no trace of curiosity or surprise at the arrival of a strange young woman at midnight as he indicated the way. Laurel followed, along a seemingly endless corridor, until José stopped. 'Here is the *sala*.' He opened an ornately panelled door and clicked a switch within, then pointed to another door at the far end of the corridor. 'If the *señorita* should wish to refresh herself she will find everything she needs.' With the grave deference of the well-trained servant he paused for any further query, then turned and faded back the way they had come.

Laurel went slowly on to the farther door, which proved to be a spacious cloakroom well equipped with a turquoise-blue tiled shower and thick fluffy towels on heated rails. The water was hot, and Laurel was tempted to indulge in a quick shower—she still felt soiled from her unpleasant experience of a short while ago—but she contented herself with washing her face and hands, and brushing away the sand that still adhered to her person. When she had done this and tidied her hair she felt slightly more human, and more presentable to return to the *sala*.

Here she was somewhat relieved to find herself in a room of rather lesser dimensions and more homely atmosphere than the great hall of the *castillo*. There were well stocked bookshelves and modern pictures, comfortable chairs for relaxing in rather than admiring their antiquity, rugs and cushions lending splashes of cool greens and warm light browns, and on a low table by the window a guitar of definitely contemporary design.

So someone in the Conde's household was musically inclined. Laurel sank into a chair, conscious of a rush of weariness that wasn't surprising after the events of the day. If only she could turn back the clock! To think that it should be the same man ... And of all men, the one on whom she had to make a good impression, for her employer's sake. She had certainly forfeited any hope of that, she thought dispiritedly, for the Conde had made no secret of his opinion of her behaviour. *Stupid juvenile folly ... foolish niña ... trespassing* ... And she had thought he pursued her like the blatant Renaldo, worse, he knew that she thought it ... Oh, if only she could turn back the clock! The swimming episode was bad enough, but tonight's misfortune ...

Laurel shivered with recollection. Thank heaven the Conde had intervened, whatever he thought of her. But if only Yvonne had not been so self-willed and foolish ...

Yvonne! The thought jolted Laurel out of her despair. She had to get back. Yvonne would be worried sick, wondering what had happened. Oh, why hadn't she insisted on returning to the guest house straight away, instead of ... Laurel sprang to her feet, and at the same moment the door opened.

She met the cool, enquiring gaze of her host.

'I—I must get back,' she stammered.

'But you have only just arrived!' One dark brow lifted. 'At least remain for the coffee which José is making.'

'Oh ... you shouldn't have bothered.' She bit her lip, wishing she knew exactly what he was thinking, and subsided back into the chair. 'It's just that it's getting so late.'

'Assignations at midnight tend to lead to that state— if nothing else,' he observed dryly.

'True, except that the assignation was not of my choosing,' she said flatly.

'Nevertheless you kept it, *señorita*.' He turned at a slight sound. 'Ah, over here, José.'

The manservant placed the tray on the table indicated and left the *sala* as quietly as he had entered. The Conde glanced at Laurel, and there was an enigmatic quality in his dark gaze.

'I believe it is the custom in your country for the *inglesa* guest to preside over the refreshments when the hostess of the house is not present? You have an odd expression for the occasion which escapes me at the moment. Perhaps you ...?'

Laurel met that mocking gaze, then got up and went to the table, determined not to supply the ridiculous phrase he obviously meant. Play mother indeed! One might as well offer to suckle a tiger! Carefully she lifted the heavy chased silver coffee pot and poured out two cups of the very black coffee. She handed one to her host. 'You appear to be well informed about our customs, *señor*,' she remarked tartly.

'I spent some time in your country a few years ago.' He thanked her with traditionally fulsome Spanish courtesy as he took the coffee, then waited until she was seated before he took a chair that directly faced hers. 'I think perhaps you are not as well versed in ours,' he added dryly.

Laurel gulped incautiously and gasped as the coffee scalded. 'What do you mean by that?'

A hint of a suppressed smiled lurked behind the gravity of his mouth. 'That is not for me to enlarge upon, *señorita*. I would not wish to cause you further embarrassment by prompting your memories of your somewhat eventful day.'

The tide of hot colour added painfully to her discomfort as those memories responded all too eagerly to the merest hint of a prompting. She averted her scarlet face, knowing she couldn't take any more of this. She lifted her cup with trembling fingers and sipped at the coffee, then she set it down and took a deep breath.

'*Señor*,' she began shakily, 'I appreciate your hospitality, and I'm deeply grateful for—for all you've done for me today, but I must get back.'

'Why?'

The uncompromising query unnerved her. 'Because it's very late,' she stammered, 'and I shouldn't be here. I—we—don't even know——'

She stopped as he began to laugh. 'What do you call late, *señorita*? You are on holiday, are you not? And the guest house does not demand that its guests be in by a certain hour, like miscreant infants!' He gestured mockingly. 'So why should you not be here? Because we have not been formally introduced? Is that what you were about to say?'

'Well, it's true! And it is rather late. I——'

'But you are not concerned about convention, surely.'

The taunt of devilry leapt in his dark eyes and his white teeth glinted. 'Oh, come, *señorita*, you do not expect me to believe that of a modern *inglesa* who swims as nature made her, and who keeps midnight trysts with a young waiter patently intent on ravishment! Surely I do not compare unfavourably with Destino's young Don Juan!'

'I never thought of making such a comparison,' she burst out wildly, 'and I do care about convention, whatever you believe, so don't run away with *that* idea. I——'

'I haven't the remotest intention of running away.' He pretended puzzlement. 'Why should I?'

'Oh, you——! I didn't mean—if you think I'm going to stay here to—to be made fun of and—and——' She clamped back on incoherencies, aware that he had reduced her to the inanities of a schoolgirl yet unable to quell the indignant rise to his needling. She took a deep breath. 'It isn't funny, *señor*, even though it seems to afford you great amusement.'

'*Señorita!*' His voice was a model of hurt dignity. 'You think that I make fun of you! Please—a thousand apologies! Command me—how can I make amends?'

Laurel closed her eyes despairingly. 'Just take things a little more seriously, and believe me when I say that tonight's tryst, as you call it, was no wish of mine.'

'No?' Suddenly the dark eyes held an intentness. 'Then how did your ring come to be in the possession of Renaldo?'

'The ring belongs to Yvonne. I wanted to get it back for her.' Laurel looked down at her hands, unwilling to make an explanation which would discredit the younger girl yet suddenly anxious to clear the somewhat dubious aura that seemed to surround herself where this man was concerned. 'I didn't think it wise for her to keep the appointment, and that's how the misunderstanding arose, *señor*.'

The Conde selected a small cheroot from a box on the table and lit it, frowning slightly. 'But wasn't that rather a strange action, *señorita*? And why did you give

Renaldo a ring which did not belong to you? Or had he stolen the ring?'

'Oh, no!' Horror clouded Laurel's eyes, and she realised she must tell him the truth, even though the little story of youthful folly seemed so inane when recounted to this dark, dominant man whose eyes had become so watchful. 'You see, *señor*, I am responsible for Yvonne. She is here because of an unsuitable friendship she formed with a man in London, and I promised her father I'd look after her. So how could I let her get involved with Renaldo? I had to try to deal with the matter myself,' she sighed.

There was a silence. After a moment Laurel looked up again, prepared for amusement, sarcasm, or mere indifference to a tale that must sound like sheer feminine imprudence, and saw instead an expression she had never expected. Sympathy!

He wafted away a thin coil of blue smoke and stubbed out the cheroot. 'She is very young, this companion?'

'Sixteen.'

He nodded. 'I know exactly how you feel, *señorita*. I too have a similar problem on my hands.'

'You?'

He betrayed a slight smile at her surprise. 'Oh, yes, *señorita*. Coping with wilful youth is not confined to your land of so-called swinging freedom. We too are meeting the problem of teenage rebellion against convention, but we, alas, find it difficult to accept so easily. Our traditions are too valued and ingrained for that.'

Laurel thought suddenly of the elderly aunt who had brought her up ever since the tragedy that had robbed her of her parents when she was little more than a baby. Aunt Adele was kind enough, and Laurel was fond of her as well as grateful, but she knew she would never shed completely some of the inhibitions instilled by an upbringing both strict and puritanical in some respects. That had been part of the trouble with Phil. He wanted more than she was prepared to give, and he couldn't understand why she said no, even though two years working in London had brought freedom with independence and a broadening of outlook undreamed-of back in the years under Aunt Adele's protective wing. Well, she had shed inhibitions with a vengeance today, and look where it had landed her!

Without realising it she sighed deeply, and the Conde, who had missed nothing of the play of expression on her oval face, leaned forward.

'You do not approve, of course. Tradition is something to be swept away, regardless of the unforeseen consequences, is it not?'

'It depends on the tradition,' she said shortly, not wishing to become involved in a discussion where she would be on shifting sand, 'and the person concerned.'

'In this case, the person concerned is young, capricious, and wayward, and completely without the wisdom to judge the worth of our tradition.'

Laurel stayed silent, and after a moment her host leaned back, his patrician features darkening in the shadows.

'My cousin is a little older than your charge, and she too has formed a misalliance of which the family greatly disapprove. A wastrel and—how do you express it?' the Conde gesticulated impatiently, 'seeker of a wealthy wife.'

'Fortune-hunter?'

'Exactly!' The Conde snapped his fingers. 'Carlota will be an extremely rich woman when she comes of age and we do not intend her to be ensnared by a *peón* who will dissipate her fortune. So she is to be removed from temptation until she returns to her senses. She arrives this coming weekend.'

'Here?'

The Conde nodded ruefully. 'I am not exactly looking forward to her visit with great joy, I'm afraid. Previously she has always been happy to be here, but now, as it is in the nature of a punishment . . .'

Laurel felt a stirring of sympathy for the unknown Carlota. 'Your cousin may be very unhappy, though,' she ventured. 'After all, she may not have known that this boy was insincere—you could even be mistaken about him.'

'Mistaken or not, the affair is ended. She will not be allowed to see him again. She will soon forget him.' The Conde's gaze rested on Laurel, a quelling power in its depths that dared her to contradict. 'A girl of seventeen does not know her own mind, let alone her heart.'

'Perhaps not,' Laurel said quietly, 'but that does not lessen her capacity for suffering.'

'So you would ally yourself to Carlota.' The considering stare probed again. 'Yet you interfere in the affairs of this young companion of yours, for her own good, naturally. You are even more inconsistent than I suspected, señorita.'

Suddenly Laurel felt weariness return. For some reason it appeared to amuse this arrogant grandee to challenge her opinions, and it was irritating, to say the least, particularly as the circumstances dictated a more tactful restraint on her part. She gave a shrug. 'I really don't know enough of the facts to ally myself with anyone, and as for my being inconsistent ... I'm sure you are too just a man to level that charge because someone doesn't agree with you.'

For a moment his dark eyes sparked, then his mouth curved unwillingly. 'Touché, señorita, perhaps I underestimate your capacity for understanding. But Carlota is scarcely in need of allies, as you will see, no doubt, when you know her a little better.'

Laurel frowned, then gave a small shake of her head. As she was unlikely to get to know Carlota it hardly mattered what she felt either way. She murmured, 'Perhaps that's so, but as it's scarcely likely to concern me ...' She stood up. 'And now, señor, I'm very tired ...'

'Of course, forgive me!' He sprang to his feet. 'I will escort you back. But first ...'

'Yes ...?' She looked at him warily as he appeared to hesitate over choice of words.

'How long is your stay on Destino to be?'

'About a month.' Laurel found difficulty in hiding

her surprise. Then a flash of panic came. Was he going to order them off the island?

'And you have been here . . . how long?'

'Less than a week—but why do you ask, *señor*?'

'For several reasons.' The dark ruthlessness first glimpsed that afternoon on the beach was again in evidence. 'You cannot remain at the guest house now, *señorita*.'

Panic fluttered again. 'But why not? I don't understand. We're booked in there for a month, with an option to stay on another two weeks . . .' A pulse flickered in her throat and she raised an unsteady hand to still its throb as she stared at his dark visage.

'Oh, surely, *señorita*.' A grimness entered his expression. 'You must realise, in view of what has happened, it would not be seemly, to say the least.'

'Seemly . . .?' She bit at her lower lip. 'I don't see——'

'Nor would it be wise,' he said grimly. 'You have been assaulted by a member of Señora Allen's staff, indirectly through the foolishness of your young charge, but nevertheless it should not have happened. I had thought Renaldo had learned his lesson after . . .' Abruptly the Conde checked, then went on: 'But rest assured, I shall deal with the culprit. I do not think he will misbehave again after he hears what I have to say to him tomorrow morning.'

Suddenly Laurel remembered, and realised the cause of the scarcely repressed anger in the man before her; he too was remembering Sara . . .

Laurel twisted her hands together nervously. Surely the Patrón could not force them to leave the island, through no fault of their own. And heaven knew what fate lay in store for Renaldo. The Master of Destino was obviously going to live up to his reputation.

She looked at him and said slowly: 'That is for you to decide, *señor*. For myself, I wish only to forget it, but I fail to see why we should be the ones to suffer. We can't cut short our holiday just because a silly incident turned from holiday flirtation into something frightening.'

'You were frightened tonight?'

'Of course I was frightened,' she said tersely, 'but not enough to remove myself just because ... no, *señor*, I can't agree. And there is nowhere else we can stay, except Mrs Allen's.'

'You will avail yourselves of my hospitality.'

'Yours?' Laurel gasped. 'You mean *here*?'

'Do not look at me as though I were insane,' he said dryly. 'Try to consider the matter from a viewpoint of logic, and think of the worry this will cause the Señora Allen to suffer when she hears of it.'

'If that's all that's worrying you she need never hear of it from me,' Laurel cried, 'nor from Yvonne. I told you, I only want to forget the whole unpleasant business, and so does Yvonne, who was worried sick over the loss of her ring. As for Renaldo, we shall certainly keep out of *his* way in future.'

'Until the next time.'

Her head came up sharply. 'What do you mean by that, *señor*?'

'Exactly what I say.' He took several paces across the room, to come to a halt before a big square mirror set in a heavily carved gilt frame. He stood there, facing her, and she saw the twin of his dark handsome head with the thick black hair that ruffled his high brow, and the long, saturnine leanness of his jaw. With a strange fascination she watched the lips in the mirror move as he went on angrily: 'I hold no brief for Renaldo, but I do not entirely blame him.'

Laurel forgot the reflection. 'Who do you blame, then?' she snapped.

'The wanton girls who play with fire and then scream when they are burnt. They flaunt themselves in little or no clothing on our beaches, seek flirtations with our men, and expect a man to turn off desire like snuffing out a candle. They do not know what they unleash, and then they wonder why a man fails to respect their womanhood.'

For a moment Laurel stared at him, wondering if she had heard aright. Did he mean that *she* ...? Because

she . . .? Outrage rose like gall in her, and she burst out:
'Are you suggesting that *I* am wanton? Just because of
something I couldn't help this afternoon? Because of
something I got involved in tonight through no fault
of my own? How dare you judge me in so insulting a
way? What right have you? Simply because you—*Oh*!
I might have expected such an attitude! Men are so
ready to condemn. They're impervious to everything
except their own arrogant opinions, and their own
desires. They are incapable of judging the character
of any woman.' She drew a deep sobbing breath, blind
now to everything but fury and the sense of injustice of
life. 'I wish I'd never set eyes on this island, and you!
Nothing—*nothing* would make me stay here after
that!'

She ran to the door, her one thought to escape, and
sobbed aloud as the blur of dark movement got there
first.

'Oh, no *señorita*, not so fast!'

He barred her way, tall, grim, and implacable. 'You
condemn me without evidence.'

'As you condemn me! Let me pass.'

'Oh, no!' Fingers of steel fastened like whiplashes
about her wrist as she tried to thrust past him. 'No
woman talks to me in that way, *señorita*, and escapes
punishment.'

'And no man talks to me as you have and gets away
with it! You're insufferable!'

Beside herself now with anger, she fought to free herself, but it was entirely by accident that one of her
flailing hands caught him across the face. He uttered
an imprecation, and the next moment she was seized
by both arms and held powerless. A strength far greater
than her own forced her arms to her sides, and dark
eyes glittered down on her distraught face. His mouth
was compressed into a thin tight line, and then suddenly his head came down and his mouth clamped on
her parted lips.

Laurel was too astounded for any reaction. The fiery
kiss locked her in time and space, quelling all ability to

move. Her senses began to swim, then she felt the hard pressure of his thighs burning through her thin garments and a choked little moan rose in her throat. And then suddenly her mouth was free.

'You foolish *chica*!' The force of the words almost brushed against her ravaged mouth. 'I suggested nothing! I did not refer to you at all—nor to your unfortunate escapade this afternoon.'

'You—you *kissed* me! You dared to——!'

'*Lex talionis!*' The angry mouth still hovered dangerously near. 'And I shall do it again if you do not apologise.'

'Apologise? Never!' She twisted her head with a desperate movement of evasion. 'You suggest I'm wanton, and then you—you force me to submit to *that*! It is you who should apologise, *señor*!'

'For what?' he hissed. 'For making a generalisation? Do you not listen? When did I specifically term you a wanton?'

'You implied it! And now you are trying to treat me like one! Let me go! You have no right to——'

'*No!*' The dark fires of anger raged in his eyes. 'Not while you revile me with unfounded accusations and your hands yearn to strike my face. I am trying to keep my temper, but you make it exceedingly difficult! Now will you listen to me, instead of spitting fury? And grant me more discernment than you credit me!'

'I'll grant you nothing while——'

'Allow me to finish what I'm endeavouring to say—please!'

Imperceptibly his tone was altering, although it was strained with the force of intensity, and the tautness in the lean lines of his features betrayed the great anger he was mastering. Something, Laurel did not know what, bade her stay silent, and he said deliberately: 'I made a generalisation, as I believe you did in your condemnation of men's motives in their treatment of a woman. But can you not realise that because of the behaviour of some—as of the young girl for whom you are responsible—you risk suffering as you did at the hands of

Renaldo? And for the very same reason *I* am classed
in the same category as young hotbloods like Renaldo!
That is the point I am endeavouring to make to you;
not a dissertation on your personal character, *señorita.*'

The Conde paused, and a sigh passed through him.
He released one of her wrists and raised his hand, to
slide a lean, curving finger along the soft curve of her
cheek. He shook his head, almost sadly.

'Foolish *chica!* Wantons do not blush! Not as you
did today— like an angry rose. As you blush even at
this moment.'

'No, I don't!' Laurel's anger was submerged in the
hot denial of embarrassment, and then she could have
bitten out her tongue for the unguarded words as she
saw the trace of a smile touch the corners of his mouth.
'Can't you forget that horrible business?' she cried. 'Or
at least allow me to forget it!'

'I am not sure I wish to forget it,' he said softly, and
the dark warmth glowing in his gaze brought a renewed surge of colour into her cheeks. 'But I promise
never to utter a mention of it again—on one condition.'

Her mouth contracted and she looked away, determined not to yield any sign of assent.

'Will you call it a pax? And promise me never to
refer again to this, shall we say, misunderstanding of
meanings?'

His hands fell away and he stepped back, watching
her with intent eyes which were now enigmatic. Laurel
gave a small, bemused shake of her head. She was unable to understand her own feelings at that moment.
Her mouth was still remembering that kiss, and her
legs were betraying a weakness that indicated sitting
down pretty soon. Strangely, she wanted to accept his
explanation, believe in his sincerity, and most of all to
say she was sorry for her own part in the angry flare
of tempers. She took a deep breath. Oh, it was ridiculous! He was charming her—she'd be eating out of
his hand in a moment! She'd be an idiot to fall for it.
But why had he changed so utterly, after all that
grandee business about punishing a woman who dared

to answer him back? She banished surmise, aware of his regard, and told herself firmly that she had to remember to be grateful to him. But for his advent tonight ...

She inclined her head. 'Very well, if you say so, *señor* ...' Her hand reached to the door, then she hesitated, turning back. 'I don't usually fly off the handle so quickly, *señor*, but today——'

'The handle?' His brows shot up. 'I do not know the idiom.'

She bit her lip, wanting to laugh suddenly, perhaps from reaction. 'I'm sorry. I meant that I don't usually jump to conclusions—angrily—so fast. But it has been a provoking day, to say the least.'

'I agree.'

She sighed, her expression grave again with weariness. She held out her hand. 'Thank you, *señor*, for coming to my aid, and the coffee, and everything. And now I think I'd better——'

She stopped. He was looking down at her with that light of mockery, the small devils tugging again at the corners of his mouth.

'The handshake of formality, *señorita*? After such a provoking day?' He shook his head. 'I will never understand the English, even if I live to be a very old man.'

He opened the door and stood back to allow her to precede him, then indicated the way. In silence she walked down the long corridor, at the end of which he opened a side door she had not noticed on her way in. It led into a small stone-floored lobby which held an assortment of sporting and fishing tackle stowed on racks, and one wall was hung with a gleaming collection of antique firearms. Laurel wondered fleetingly if the *castillo* possessed its quota of dungeons, and then the Conde was opening the heavy studded outer door. It gave on to a large courtyard, dimly illuminated by ancient iron basket lanterns, and nearby was a green coupé to which the Conde strode and opened the passenger door.

Laurel got in and looked around. It was impossible not to be fascinated by the scene. The moon was high now, casting inky black shadows and outlining the high, fretted stone battlements and gothic towers, and the broad archway in the outer wall framed velvet midnight sky and a silver flash of shimmering sea.

The journey took only minutes by car, and Laurel felt a twinge of regret that it was over so soon; the island was so very lovely by moonlight, and the narrow winding road from the little port up to the guest house that had become familiar by day took on a new strangeness when traversed in the moonlight by car. The Conde drew to a smooth stop at the gate to the guest house. He turned to her.

'You sigh, *señorita*. You must be extremely tired—I regret that I have delayed you over late.'

'No—I sighed because it's so beautiful.' Laurel hesitated. 'I trust you were not serious about—about our leaving Destino?'

'But I never suggested you should leave the island.' He sounded surprised. 'I stated that you and your companion could not remain where you are. And I meant every word of it,' he added flatly.

'You mean that we ...?'

He leaned back, one hand still curved reflectively over the top of the wheel. 'It occurs to me that some feminine companionship would not come amiss during my cousin's visit to Destino. *Doña* Costenza—my aunt —is at present with friends in Granada, and she will not take kindly to curtailing her visit in order to return here to look after Carlota. Unfortunately,' he sighed, 'I have business to attend to in Madrid which I can't defer, and although it should not keep me away more than a matter of days, it means Carlota will be left to her own devices here. My grandmother is too frail and infirm to be irked by Carlota's rebellious and unpredictable tantrums.'

Laurel was silent, and he went on: 'Who knows? I may even return to find that Carlota has seized the opportunity to return to her forbidden amour. I should not care to be responsible for providing that excuse.'

'Yes, I see. It's quite a problem, if she is as self-willed

as you say,' Laurel said slowly. 'But do you think the presence of strangers will make any difference?'

'Oh, yes. The presence of guests, with the necessity of her taking the strain of a hostess's duties from my grandmother's shoulders, will compel her to remain. So please, *señorita*, consider the matter. Your acceptance of my invitation will solve both problems. And remember, if you decline, Renaldo must be removed immediately from his post. I will not permit him to remain there near a young girl as impressionable as your charge appears to be, and certainly not near one as rudely abused as yourself. But this will sadly inconvenience Señora Allen, and a replacement in her staff may be difficult to arrange at this particular time.'

'Would it?' Laurel was not entirely convinced. 'I shouldn't have thought so.'

'You do not know my island, nor its labour resources; still less the capabilities of those resources. Therefore you will permit me to deal with these matters as I think fit.'

'Of course, *señor*,' she said hastily, 'but there is the financial side to consider. I don't know what to do about that— I mean, we've already paid for our accommodation, at least part of it, and what about Mrs Allen? It's not fair that she should lose out over this.'

He shocked her by laughing out loud. 'Mrs Allen will not lose by it, nor will you, my obstinate little *inglesa*. And *I* will feel a great deal happier to know that you are safely in my care. For, if you will forgive me saying so, I fear you are somewhat accident-prone, and goodness knows what else may happen to you before your stay on Destino reaches its close.'

Laurel bit back an indignant retort; accident-prone indeed! But the time for anger was over; he seemed genuinely concerned for her welfare and very generous with his offer of hospitality—even though he had been frank about the reason for it and that it would suit his own purpose. But she did not know what to say. The last thing she had expected was an invitation to stay at the *castillo*.

Aware that he was waiting, she said at last, 'This is all very kind of you, *señor*, and I am already indebted to you, but surely it is not necessary that you should feel bound to assume responsibility for two strangers. And as far as your cousin is concerned, well,' she hesitated awkwardly, 'we would be delighted to meet her and—and help in any way we can to prevent her from feeling lonely.'

'*Señorita!*' He slewed round to face her, and all the disarming charm of a few moments ago had vanished. Once again those dark eyes glittered with anger. 'I believe I have already disclaimed all knowledge of any debt. But it seems you are not convinced! Or is it merely that the English must for ever protest, lest something be proffered from empty politeness?'

'No, of course not!' Laurel recoiled from the aura of sheer power this man could exude. 'Please don't think I——'

'Listen to me, *señorita*. We too have our set of social mores. As we left my home I might have said to you: *Ya sabe usted donde tiene su casa!* Not to do so could cause affront to a guest used to our formalities. But tell me, *señorita*, where during our discussions this night have I ever conveyed a sense of mere empty pleasantries not worth the breath expended upon them?'

Laurel restrained a gasp of dismay. Could she never say the right thing? She looked at him wearily and shook her head. 'No, *señor*, never. Oh, try to understand. It's true—we do protest from a sense of politeness. And I do know of the pleasantry about taking possession of your home, which surely answers the question. I have to make sure I do not presume too much.' She sighed and looked down at her hands, trying to still their nervous movements. 'But it seems I only succeed in offending you, *señor*, which is the last thing I wish to do.'

There was a small silence. Then he reached over and touched her hand. 'I think in my heart I am aware of that. And now I have detained you quite long enough.

Tomorrow I will call upon you and all will be resolved.'

He raised her hand and touched his lips to it, and Laurel wondered if she were dreaming. Less than half an hour since he kissed her in violent anger and taunted her for the conventional reactions; now he was utterly formal, quickly leaving the car and handing her out, escorting her to the shadowed entrance and making a brief mocking salute with a whispered '*Adiós*—we must not disturb the sleeping colonels!' and then slipping back into the darkness.

Laurel listened to the fading sounds of the car before she let herself quietly into the silent house. Suddenly she was aware of a distinct shakiness and a feeling of lightheaded unreality. It seemed aeons since this morning when she had set out to explore the island. The Conde had been only a name then; now he seemed to have filled her entire horizon ... Unless it had all been a dream ...

'*Laurel!* Where *have* you been?'

Yvonne sped down from the shadows under the dim light that burned all night on the staircase. Her face was white with strain, and almost accusing as she reached the hall and faced Laurel.

'I've just about been out of my mind! Who was that? I saw the car and thought ...' She did not give Laurel time to reply and held out her hand. 'Did you get it?'

For a moment Laurel stared blankly at her, then almost hysterical mirth came as she remembered. The ring! The cause of all the trouble.

The Conde still had the ring.

CHAPTER FIVE

'Did he say definitely what time he would call?'

'No.' Laurel replaced the cap on her toothpaste tube and ran water into the washbasin. 'He simply said he would call tomorrow—that's today,' she added with a trace of tiredness.

'But what if he doesn't?' Yvonne inspected her eyelashes, then pouted into the mirror. 'What if I don't get that ring back? Honestly, Laurie, you're the limit. I can't think how you could forget to ask for it.'

'Because I'd had enough to cope with for one day.' Laurel lost patience as she groped for the towel. 'I'd had one row with him, and then.... All I wanted was to get back here. Fending off your Lothario wasn't exactly a picnic.'

'I say!' Yvonne forgot her grievance for a moment and a gleam came into her eyes. 'Was it true? Did he really?'

'Really what? Rape me?'

'Yes—well, if what's-his-name had to rescue you ...'

'He had a jolly good try,' Laurel said dryly. 'Just make sure *you* keep out of Renaldo's way in future.'

'Golly!' Yvonne's eyes rounded. 'I wasn't sure whether you were having me on or not last night. But you must have led him on a bit.'

'I did *not* lead him on,' Laurel said bitterly, turning away to drape the towel over the rail.

Yvonne waited, then said hopefully, 'Aren't you going to tell me?'

'I told you last night.'

'You didn't! Not properly.'

'If you're after salacious details you won't get them from me,' Laurel said flatly. 'I want to forget the whole unpleasant business.'

'Oh, you are mean!' Yvonne pouted again. Then her eyes brightened dreamily. 'All the same, it must have been exciting—being rescued at midnight by a stranger, a real Spanish count, on a great black horse, and carried off to his castle.' She sighed. 'Some people have all the luck!'

'It was luck—and excitement— I could well have done without,' Laurel said tartly. Refusing to be drawn into any further appeasement of Yvonne's curiosity, she began to dress. The shadows beneath her eyes betrayed the strain of the previous day and the night's lack of sleep, for it had been well after two before Yvonne allowed her to settle down, and by then she was in that highly strung state when sleep becomes unattainable. The events of the day, culminating in the disastrous encounter with Renaldo followed by its unexpected sequel, had chased through her mind like a feverish dream. She had tossed and turned, and the last time she had looked despairingly at the little glowing dial of her watch it had said ten past five. After that, she had at last drifted into a heavy sleep from which she was awakened, anything but refreshed, by the little maid bringing in the morning cup of tea. Now, remembered in the bright clear light of morning, it all seemed like a dream, the most disturbing, exhausting dream of all time. But Yvonne had no intention of allowing dreams to fade.

All through breakfast she persisted with questions.

'Are we really going to stay at the *castillo*?'

'I don't know.'

'But if he's invited us ...'

'I don't know if we'd be wise to accept.'

'But why not? *I* want to! I think it's a super idea.' Yvonne leaned eagerly across the table. 'You still haven't told me what he's like. Is he young?'

'I didn't ask him his age,' Laurel snapped, then instantly repented as Yvonne looked hurt. 'I should imagine he's somewhere in his early thirties. He's not a youth like Renaldo.'

'Oh.' Yvonne wrinkled her nose. 'He's older. Is he good to look at? You know, warm and dark and sort of velvety, like Renaldo?'

'I wouldn't describe him in the same breath.' Laurel's mouth tightened. She supposed the Conde was an extremely handsome man, if one liked his particularly dangerous kind of looks. And as for comparing him to Renaldo ... it was like comparing a ran-tan young alley tom with a pure-bred tiger; a tiger in velvet ... Suddenly she felt a strange reluctance to start trying to describe his physical characteristics to the avid Yvonne. She could not trust herself to remain completely cool and apparently indifferent. 'There's no comparison,' she said tersely. 'Anyway, you'll probably see for yourself soon.'

'I've always wanted to stay in a castle,' Yvonne murmured dreamily, then remembered something. She looked up sharply. 'Hey, you said something about having a row with him. When? What for?'

Laurel bitterly regretted her careless tongue. She had no intention of enlightening Yvonne about that fiery exchange in the *sala* of the *castillo* last night, and even less of confiding the sorry little tale of her first, mortifying encounter with the autocrat of Destino. She said evenly, 'I was exaggerating a bit. Like you, the Conde seemed to imagine that I must have given Renaldo some encouragement. So I had to disabuse him of that notion. I don't think he's used to being answered back,' she added wryly.

'Was that all?'

'I think it was enough.' Laurel decided it was high time the subject was changed. 'Are you feeling better this morning?'

'Me? Oh, yes, I'm fine now.' Yvonne appeared to have forgotten her indisposition of the previous evening. 'Do I look all right?'

'Perfect!' Laurel responded instantly to the anxiety in the younger girl's expression. She smiled ruefully. 'If I felt half as good as you look at the moment I'd be quite content.'

Yvonne looked surprised. 'But you always look super, Laurie. Sort of cool and beautiful and serene. I've always wished I could look like that,' she said in one of her endearing moments of candidness, 'but it never works out right for me.'

It was Laurel's turn to betray surprise. The unexpected compliment was heartwarming. She said gently, 'You have no cause for worry on that score, Yvonne. You've plenty of appeal of your own. When you are a little older and have learned to exploit your full potential you'll never need to envy other girls. They'll envy you.'

'Will they really?'

'They most certainly will.' Laurel finished her coffee and smiled. 'I'm going to laze in the garden for a while. What are you going to do?'

'Laze with you—and wait for the king of the castle. I'm longing to see him.'

In this new mood of rapport the two girls took their books and sun-glasses out into the morning sunshine. But Yvonne's longing was not to be fulfilled. There was no summons before lunch time, and after lunch she began to fret again about the missing ring. All Laurel's assurances that the ring would be perfectly safe failed to banish the anxious cloud from Yvonne's brow, and at last she had to promise that they would walk up to the *castillo* that evening, should the Conde not have fulfilled his promise before then.

After lunch the terrace soon echoed gently to the snores of Colonel Carlton and Mr Binkley. Mrs Carlton and Mrs Binkley were discussing crochet patterns, and Mr Jamieson, in a pair of very baggy khaki shorts which by the kindest of criterions hardly enhanced his large paunch and pallid matchstick legs, was practising swings with an imaginary club and bemoaning the lack of golfing facilities on Destino.

'He's off again,' groaned Yvonne under her breath. 'Why doesn't he go to Gleneagles? Laurie, will you stay? Even if I miss him I can't face an afternoon of this.'

'Where are you going?'

'The beach—there might be somebody there. I won't be long.'

She loped away, lithe and slender in brief scarlet shorts and a tiny cheesecloth smock dotted with blue florets, and Mr Jamieson paused to watch her with an old man's shameless eyes. Laurel sighed as she turned away, hoping there wouldn't be anyone on the beach, at least anyone like Renaldo! But what could she do? She couldn't keep tabs on Yvonne every minute of the day, even if she wished to, for it was no more pleasant being gaoler than captive. Perhaps the Conde was right; the *castillo* was the best place for Yvonne, if not herself. There, Yvonne would be more likely to be on her best behaviour, as the idea seemed to have caught her interest, and if Carlota proved amenable there was the possibility of a new friendship which might help to alleviate Yvonne's scarcely contained boredom. In her heart Laurel could not blame the younger girl for feeling as she did. At present the island, lovely as it was, belonged strictly to its own people. They welcomed visitors—provided those visitors accepted Destino and its unchanging tradition on its own terms. For someone like Yvonne a holiday there could seem a very tame affair indeed. Suddenly she found herself hoping that the Conde's invitation had not been an idle one and that he would remember his promise to call ...

With the intention of collecting her writing case from their room and then seeking the side terrace, where it would be cooler and shaded, Laurel entered the house and immediately encountered Miss Jessops.

The gentle, lonely little woman always sparked a feeling of compassion in Laurel and she paused to exchange pleasantries before going upstairs. When she returned Miss Jessops was still there, poring over the view postcards displayed in a rack near the reception desk. She blinked nervously at Laurel.

'I still forget about this siesta time. Do you think it'll be all right if I help myself to a few cards—I don't want to disturb Mrs Allen?'

Laurel smiled. 'I'm sure it'll be all right. I'm choosing a couple and I think I'll just leave the money in this bowl.'

Miss Jessops did the same, and it was inevitable that she should follow Laurel out to the terrace where the wide awning deflected the direct heat of the sun and let the light breeze be pleasantly cool.

Miss Jessops said suddenly, 'Has your friend deserted you?'

'Oh——' Laurel glanced up—'just for a while. She's gone down to the beach.'

Miss Jessops nodded. 'I'm afraid she's finding us dull company. It's natural, I suppose. All the same,' she sighed and gave a rueful smile, 'it amuses me sometimes the way the youngsters today seem to imagine we never lived. Emmie and I used to have such fun. I'll never forget the Boat Race Night when Reggie threw Freddie into the fountain. He was a devil! Emmie could have married him, but she didn't love him. Then she went crazy over a young Frenchman we met in Nice. He and his friend followed us for miles, simply miles, along the Promenade des Anglais, and we were trying to pretend they weren't there. Because of course in those days it was considered quite daring for nice girls to allow themselves to be picked up. Emmie's mother would have been shocked to the core if she'd ever found out. Oh, that was a wonderful holiday ...' Miss Jessops sighed deeply. 'It was the year the war broke out, and afterwards it was never quite the same. Freddie never came back. We were going to be married on his next leave, and then ... he never came back from Dunkirk.'

'I'm sorry,' murmured Laurel.

'It was like the end of the world; except that I had to go on living ...'

A bee drowsed lazily in the blossoms near where Laurel sat, drugged with nectar and the sun, and an unseen bird rustled and twittered among the creepers while Miss Jessops plucked the memories of bygone years and peopled the terrace with the ghosts from her past, some sad, some happy, but strangely evocative. Until she stopped, her eyes clouding with guilt.

'My dear, I must be boring you to extinction. Forgive me.'

'There's nothing to forgive. And I'm certainly not bored.' Laurel was being perfectly truthful. Miss Jessops had a beautifully modulated diction and also the raconteur's gift for selecting the more telling items from her far from dull life, once she was given a willing listener, and somehow she brought to life the essence of a decade that began a turning point in history.

'You are too accommodating, my dear! I'm not going to say another word!'

Miss Jessops applied herself to the writing of her cards, and for a little while there was silence, until the others began to drift round from the garden. It was getting near to four, and Mrs Allen kept true to the tradition of afternoon tea for those of her guests who wished it, invariably serving it on the side terrace.

Somewhat to Laurel's surprise Yvonne landed back just as the trolley was being wheeled through the dining room towards the sliding doors that gave out on to the terrace.

She plumped herself down into a chair and fanned herself, pulling a meaning grimace at Laurel. Tactfully, Laurel ignored it, and Miss Jessops enquired innocently if Yvonne had had a nice afternoon.

'You're joking!' Yvonne heaved a sigh of disgust, and Miss Jessops, with a sympathetic smile at the girl, rose to go towards the far end of the terrace, where the tea trolley now stood.

It was the custom for the guests to help themselves to the dainty sandwiches, tiny scones and little cakes which Mrs Allen herself baked freshly each day, and which vanished remarkably quickly in spite of the show of languid reluctance with which the guests gathered round the trolley to select their fancy.

'Just look at them,' said Yvonne. 'They positively live from one meal to the next in this place. But of course they haven't much else to live for, poor dears.'

'*Yvonne!*' remonstrated Laurel in a shocked whisper. 'Keep your voice down—if you must make such unkind remarks.'

'Well, it's true.' Yvonne had the grace to lower her voice. 'I didn't mean it that way.'

'Then perhaps it might be better in future to make such frank observations with a little more discretion, *señorita*.'

The cool, reproving tones brought both girls' heads sharply round to the newcomer. Laurel's hand fluttered up to her throat as she encountered the dark mocking gaze that was beginning to haunt her both waking and sleeping. How long had he stood there? How had she not heard him come through the patio doors to stand immediately behind her chair? But Yvonne betrayed no such giveaway gesture after her first start of surprise. She stared back at him with resentful young eyes.

'I don't usually make confidential remarks to strangers—especially if I know they're listening,' she said pointedly.

Laurel's heart gave a lurch of dismay. She started to rise, but the Conde was not looking at her. His gaze was on Yvonne's indignant face, and suddenly he smiled.

'Forgive me, *señorita*—my lapse is far greater than your own. Allow me ...' He reached for Yvonne's hand and raised it to his lips. 'Rodrigo de Renzi, at your service. And you, *señorita*, must be....'

Yvonne whispered her name, visibly warming to the dark, arrogant charm now turned full on her, and remembered to withdraw her hand from his clasp. She smiled beguilingly up into his face and said, 'I'll forgive you, *señor*—you know I did not intend offence.'

He inclined his head gravely. 'I am sure of it, *señorita*. Alas, when one grows old there is often little left than appreciation of good food and wine, but one does not expect such perception from one so youthful.'

At last he seemed to remember Laurel's presence. He said, 'May I join you?'

'Of course.' Painfully aware that her poise had deserted her, Laurel sank back into her chair. How easily Yvonne was talking to him, all trace of her former boredom vanished and a warm vitality lighting her features and glowing in her eyes. She was basking in the sheer pleasure of monopolising the attention of the most attractive male within miles, and already the Conde was taking the serpent ring from his pocket in response to her sudden appealing enquiry.

He leaned forward, murmuring that she should take care to place it somewhere safe, and she reached out one small slender hand. 'My finger would be the safest, I think!'

He smiled, his dark brows quirking. 'May I?'

Yvonne fluttered and giggled as he slid the ring on to her finger, then thanked him for restoring her property, adding in her uninhibited way that her father would have half-killed her if she'd lost it.

Laurel tried to restrain a cynical smile at this last extravagance—Mr Searle was the last man to fit the stern Victorian father image—then she forgot her employer as the Conde's gaze swung to her face.

He said, 'It is not me you should thank, *señorita*. It is your friend to whom you owe the return of your ring.'

'Oh, yes,' Yvonne said carelessly, 'poor Laurie got quite involved last night, I gather.'

'Yes—poor Laurie, indeed.' His eyes had gone grave again and there was no more mockery in their dark depths. 'I trust you are quite recovered from your distressing experiences of yesterday, *señorita*?'

She nodded, aware of a strange little pang at hearing the diminutive of her name on his lips for the first time. 'Would you care for some tea?' she asked, belatedly remembering the eating and drinking that was going on in their vicinity.

'Thank you, but it is already arranged, and I have also talked with Mrs Allen about the matter we discussed last evening.' He paused. 'She is in complete agreement with me. All that remains is to await your own assent, *señoritas*, and arrange a suitable time for your journey to the *castillo*.'

Yvonne's eyes sparkled, and Laurel tried to quell the small, persistent doubt that still persisted in its niggling. If only she could be sure they were doing the right thing in allowing the Conde to manage their affairs this way. Yet if Mrs Allen now knew and had agreed ...

Rosita arrived at that moment, wheeling the smaller trolley on which reposed a most attractive setting for afternoon tea. Yvonne made a small moue and whispered that this was sheer favouritism, which, judging by the surprised glances of the other guests, it was, and the Conde crossed elegantly clad knees, looking perfectly at home at Rosita handed round tea in the fragile bone china that was so essentially English despite the exotic setting. *The man's a positive chameleon,* Laurel thought. He could fit in anywhere, and Yvonne was completely won.

She sipped her tea and tried resolutely to banish her doubts. When the news got round the guest house, as it did within moments of the Conde's departure, the general opinion seemed to be that she and Yvonne were two especially favoured and fortunate girls actually to be invited to stay at the home of none other than the master of Destino himself. But strangely, the one reason for genuine doubt did not even enter Laurel's mind as she packed her things and prepared to leave with Yvonne when the Conde's car arrived at the appointed hour that evening to take them to Castillo Valderosa.

By the time the car entered the great gates and swept up to the imposing entrance some of Yvonne's elation had infected Laurel, and she was conscious of a quickening heartbeat when she stepped out of the car and the Conde came forward to bid her welcome.

He suggested the two girls might prefer to be shown to their rooms first and then rejoin him a little later for an aperitif. 'We shall be dining at nine this evening,' he added, 'but quite informally while Doña Costenza is away.'

'I wonder what his idea is of informality,' Yvonne murmured, once they were alone together in the spacious bedroom that had been allotted to Laurel. 'Do we roll down in jeans or full regalia?'

'I'm playing safe with my velvet skirt and lace top.'

'Mm, shall I wear my new gear—I haven't dared wear it so far?' Yvonne smiled wickedly. 'Why not? Let's give His Majesty a treat. Perhaps he needs it if he has to suffer eating with an autocratic old aunt all the time.'

Laurel's expression at the thought of Yvonne's long slim legs whisking down to dinner beneath the semi-transparent skirts of the red and black creation so disapproved by her father was enough to send Yvonne into peals of mirth. 'Don't worry—I was only teasing,' she cried. 'Isn't it super having our own rooms? Come and see mine—it's like a young ballroom, and I've got my own balcony overlooking the sea.'

Certainly the bedrooms were luxurious and furnished with both taste and thoughtfulness for a guest's every need. Laurel's had silver-grey wall-to-wall carpet, deep rose curtains and quilt, white and gilt fitted furniture against a pale rose and silver striped wallpaper, and an onyx vanity unit with big crystal taps, while Yvonne's was laid out in a similar pattern, but this time in lime green, silver and palest primrose.

'I expected black oak and fourposters, and ancient conquistadors leering down from the walls,' Yvonne giggled. 'Though I think there'll be lots of that downstairs, judging by ye olde baronial hall where we came in. I say, Laurie,' she turned from the wardrobe, 'wouldn't this make a super hotel for Daddy's tours?'

Laurel gave a stifled exclamation, and Yvonne stared. 'What's the matter?'

The dress on its hanger still over her arm, Yvonne took a step towards Laurel, who had sunk on to the end of the bed, her face clouded with dismay. Laurel looked up at the younger girl. 'I'd forgotten! How on earth could I forget that?'

Yvonne frowned. 'Forget what?'

'The job. My work for your father.'

Puzzlement increased in Yvonne's eyes. 'But you haven't forgotten! What do you mean?'

Laurel shook her head, almost as though she did not hear. 'How on earth am I going to tell him?'

Yvonne stared at her, then suddenly comprehension flooded her face. 'You mean the Conde? You mean you haven't told him why we're here on Destino?'

'No,' Laurel groaned. 'So much has happened the last two days it just went right out of my head. Heavens, what am I going to do? I mean, how does one suddenly break the news to one's host that one's virtually spying out the lie of his land?'

Yvonne drew a deep breath and went to hang up the dress in her wardrobe, then she came back to where Laurel still sat. 'You can't,' she said simply.

'Can't? I must! I've no other alternative.'

'Yes, you have. Don't say a word.' Yvonne leaned forward earnestly. 'Don't you see, it's a marvellous opportunity—it couldn't have worked out better. Being his guests, he'll talk to us, show us round, tell us everything we want to know. Think of the trouble it'll save.'

'Yvonne! I couldn't! It would be deliberate deception.'

'Not really. After all, it might turn out to be another of Daddy's non-starters. So the Conde wouldn't know in any case.'

'I still can't let him think I'm just an ordinary tourist. No,' Laurel stood up and paced to the window, 'I'll tell him when we go down. What he'll say, I hate to think.'

Yvonne's sigh was clearly audible. 'I thought it was too good to be true. Well, I guess I'd better start shoving these back into my case.'

Laurel made no reply, and after a moment the younger girl crossed the room and touched her shoulder. 'Laurie . . .'

'Yes?'

'Does a stranger really mean more to you than Daddy and me?'

'No, of course not!' Laurel swung round fiercely. 'Can't you see, it isn't a case of who means more to me —I hope I'll always be loyal to your father—but I can't deceive a man who has offered us hospitality, not in this unusual circumstance.'

'Listen, it *isn't* as bad as you think,' Yvonne protested. 'The Conde isn't having us here simply out of the goodness of his heart, Laurie. He has an axe of his own to grind. He needs somebody to amuse his wayward cousin, doesn't he? And we happened to be handy. So doesn't that cancel out our side of the business?'

'Oh, it isn't as easy as that, Yvonne. I wish it were.'

Yvonne looked at her troubled face and gave a shrug of despair. 'I suppose you're right. But I don't know what Daddy's going to say when we land home and say it's all off.'

Laurel's head jerked round. She was beginning to comprehend Yvonne's line of thought and the dismay of realisation showed plainly in her eyes. Yvonne stared back grimly.

'You didn't think we could go back to Mrs Allen's, did you?' she cried. 'Once he knows we'll have to leave the island, never mind the *castillo*. And Daddy's going to want to know why. And I'll have to tell him. He'll say it's all my fault!'

'But it isn't!' Amazement chased dismay from Laurel's face. 'How could you know it would turn out like this?'

'It is my fault.' The tears began to glisten in Yvonne's eyes. 'If it hadn't been for me and my silly ring, and Renaldo, and everything, none of this would have happened. And it's no use saying you won't tell Daddy,' she cried bitterly, 'because he'll know that I was to blame without being told. And—well, I've caused him enough trouble lately, I suppose.'

Her shoulders began to tremble, and she groped towards the container on the dressing table for a tissue. She blew her nose and sniffed miserably. 'I don't think I want to go down to dinner, Laurie.'

Laurel closed her eyes despairingly. If only there were some way out of this impasse! Whichever course she chose would lead to trouble. Yvonne had pointed out the very real risk that the truth would bring, for almost certainly the Conde would ask them to leave

the island. Laurel had only to remember his anger and
his high-handed attitude towards herself when she had
literally plunged into disaster the previous afternoon.
Just the memory was enough to suffuse her cheeks with
the crimson of shame; and then last night ... He certainly had left her in no doubt as to his opinion of
girls who flouted his own rules of convention. And
then there was her employer to consider. He would be
hurt and disappointed if she landed back to report
failure.

Laurel sighed and dragged herself back to the
present. She said firmly, 'You must come down to
dinner, Yvonne, even if only out of courtesy to our
host and not because I'll have to face it and him by
myself.'

'Are—are you going to tell him?'

'I—I don't know.' Laurel moved towards the door.
'I'll have to think it over.'

'Promise you won't blurt it out while I'm there?
Because it'd be even worse for me,' Yvonne begged. 'It's
my father who wants to develop the island for tourism
—after all, you're simply following orders.'

Yvonne looked so woebegone Laurel could only nod
and give the required promise, but her heart was
heavy when eventually she and Yvonne went downstairs
and were shown into the vast *sala* where the Conde
awaited. It went against every principle Laurel had
been taught, and yet if she did not stay silent she
could cause a chain reaction in Mr Searle's plans. And
Yvonne's mother was in such poor health ...

If the Conde had chosen to live up to the first, daunting impressions Laurel had received it might have made
it easier for her to be swayed towards Yvonne's way of
thinking, but he didn't. It was almost as though he
set out deliberately to charm, even enchant his two
young guests. There was wine and soft music in the
gracious room, and then a leisurely meal in the candle-
lit dining hall, a great panelled place of mellow old
furniture, gleaming with centuries of polishing, and
finely chased silver, and superb food served by a soft-

footed manservant in black. There was iced melon, a
seafood salad, little potato curls and tender flaking
croquettes, an apricot flambé, and then cheeses and
fruit and coffee, and finally liqueurs to set the seal on
a magnificent feast.

The scene held a dreamlike quality, Laurel reflected.
The Conde looked more handsome than ever in dark
evening clothes, a moiré silk cummerbund and white
ruffled shirt enhancing his Latin elegance and dark
features, and the occasional flickers of the candlelight
lent an air of mysticism that was dangerously fascinat-
ing. He told them that his grandmother, the aged Condesa, sent them her greetings of welcome and hoped to
have the pleasure of meeting the two girls the following morning.

'She is very frail, and at times finds the evening meal
beyond her strength,' he explained. 'Of late she keeps
more and more to her own suite where Maria guards
and cossets her like a child.'

He offered no further information, and Laurel wondered how many more members of the Conde's family
lived at the *castillo*. How would they receive the two
strangers he had chosen to invite under his roof? But
no such doubt seemed to trouble Yvonne as they moved
out to the terrace, there to watch the lights winking
down in the little port and the great silver moon rising
over the sea. The Conde made conversation easily, en-
couraging Yvonne to blossom forth vivaciously, and
apparently not noticing that Laurel was still strained
and withdrawn.

It was after midnight when the Conde glanced at his
watch and exclaimed with seeming reluctance, 'I fear
I have monopolised your evening—you will wish to
unpack and settle in. Forgive me.'

He escorted them to the foot of the broad staircase
and bade them a courteous goodnight. The girls began
to ascend, Yvonne a stair or two ahead of Laurel, and
then the Conde's attractively accented voice came suddenly:

'Miss Daneway—*perdone usted*—there is something I forget!'

She stopped, aware of Yvonne also pausing, and then realising that he wished her to rejoin him she went slowly down to where he waited.

He indicated a broad panelled doorway directly to his right, and after a moment of hesitation she obeyed the gesture which bade her enter. Again she was conscious of the quickening of her heartbeat and something like fear as he followed her into the large book-lined room and closed the door. Now what was wrong? What had she said or done?

'*Señorita*, does something trouble you?' he asked without preamble.

Laurel started. 'N-no, Señor Conde. Why do you ask?'

'You seemed unusually quiet this evening.'

'Was I? It—it wasn't intentional,' she said awkwardly.

His brows arched slightly. 'I wondered if perhaps I had offended you in some way?'

This was the return to *la galanteria*—though the air of enquiry was strongly defined—and Laurel felt puzzled. Perhaps it was her guilty conscience, but she almost preferred his anger and his arrogance to this display of the traditional suave gallant, at least to that she could retort with spirit and know where she stood. She said warily, 'How could you offend me, *señor*? On the contrary, I am overwhelmed by your hospitality. You have spared nothing for our welcome.'

'That is as it should be.' His dark head was proud and erect, every inch of him the grandee who would take it as a personal affront were his guests to find his hospitality wanting in the minutest respect. 'I wish your stay with us to be as pleasant as it is within my power to make it. That is why tonight I feel concerned that something seems not—not as it should be, *señorita*.'

He waited, his gaze compelling her to meet its intensity, and the tight knot of tension within Laurel hardened its grip. The cold prompting of conscience told her that this was the moment to tell him the truth behind her presence on the island, that if she allowed this opportunity to pass there might never be another. She struggled to frame words with which to begin, and saw his expression change. The mocking lights began to dance in the dark eyes and the quirks touched the corners of the handsome, sensuous mouth.

'Come, *chica*, there is nothing to be afraid of! Where is that fighting spirit that flared to attack me from all sides yesterday?' The quirks gave way to a smile in which the now familiar devilry lurked. 'Or is it that you feel bowed down by responsibility for your charming companion and the need to be on your best behaviour?'

'Perhaps,' said Laurel tonelessly. The moment had gone, and in its place came the pricking of danger signals. She had known this man for little more than twenty-four hours, but already she recognised the complex facets of his personality. He would stimulate her into retaliation, she would say things she would bitterly regret afterwards, and his mocking air of teasing would fire rapidly into anger.

He still smiled. 'We are human, *señorita*, and I at least do not expect an English girl to don the airs of her Spanish counterpart.'

She shook her head. 'I would not dream of attempting to do so, *señor*. But I can only hope that you will find your first impressions of me prove false. I would be a poor guest who wished to attack so generous a host.'

'So,' his shoulders moved slightly, 'no sparks, *señorita*?'

'No sparks,' she said flatly.

He turned away slightly and glanced up at an age-mellowed portrait of a brooding-visaged ancestor in whose painted eyes there dwelled a certain recognisable light. The Conde's lips twitched. 'It seems I forge my rapier to no account!'

Laurel had followed the direction of his gaze. 'If you consider a weapon essential, I'm afraid so.'

'*Señorita*, I am devastated!'

Suddenly Laurel's eyes stung and she could not meet the challenge she saw in his lean features. 'Surely not by so untempered an opponent, *señor*.'

'Do not underrate yourself, *chica*!' he exclaimed. 'There is a certain steel beneath the softness of a woman which can render a man's weapons useless.'

Laurel sighed. 'Perhaps you speak from experience, *señor*. I assure you, I have no desire either to fence with words or cross swords, and certainly not to hide beneath a feminine softness.'

'I should be disappointed if you did.' He moved towards her and looked down at her averted face. 'But do not challenge me with talk of experience, *señorita*, lest I be tempted to a *sentiment du fer*.'

Laurel could only guess that the expression was a technical fencing term, and one it might be foolish to attempt to parry with ignorance. She looked up at him and tried to instil lightness into her tone. 'Do you always challenge your guests to a duel, *señor*?'

'Only if I consider them worthy of my mettle.'

The wave of sadness washed over her again and she turned away wearily, no longer caring if he chose to construe the movement as discourteous. 'I think you are making fun of me again, *señor*.'

There was a brief silence, then the sound of a lithe movement behind her before warm hands closed on her shoulders. She felt the slight drift of his breath stir a wisp of her hair, then he whispered, '*Never*!'

An inexplicable shudder coursed through Laurel's body and brought with it a vivid memory of that bruising, fiery kiss of last night. She felt his hands begin to turn her, as though to face him, and the wild, disturbing agitation caused by his nearness made her twist free to put the distance of safety between herself and this enigmatic man. Hardly knowing what she was saying she stammered, 'I—I hope I have answered your question, *señor* . . .'

'Ah yes . . .' Perceptibly he changed, the cool mask of courtesy reforming, as he drew himself to his full height. 'Once again I forget and detain you, *señorita*. A thousand pardons ...'

He reached out with one hand to open the door for her, but in the second before she moved he had caught and imprisoned the slender fingers that plucked nervously at the froth of lace at the throat of her evening blouse. He drew them to his lips, retaining them within the warmth of his own for a fraction of time more than necessary, then released them and stepped back.

Laurel inclined her head, murmuring a goodnight in a voice that didn't seem to belong to her, then walked unsteadily out of the room. All the way up the wide staircase she was conscious of him standing down there in the hall, watching her ascent, and all the time she was aware of a strange mingling of emotions making her heart thud breathlessly in her breast. A sense of elation fighting to be free, and oppressing it a sadness that she dared not begin to explain ...

CHAPTER SIX

'MM, this is what I call the good life!'

Yvonne stretched luxuriously and studied the gleaming rose lacquer she had just applied to her well-shaped nails. 'What say you, *bella* Laurie?'

Laurel smiled indulgently. 'You're becoming quite a little lotus-eater, aren't you? Enjoying your riding sessions?'

'What do you think?' Yvonne grinned. 'Enjoying your poetry sessions with the Condesa?'

'Actually she's a very sweet old lady. It's a shame her arthritis is so bad.'

'Yes,' said Yvonne carelessly, blowing gently on the drying lacquer, 'she seems to have taken a liking to you.'

Laurel shrugged. 'I think she's lonely—and whatever age has done to her it hasn't impaired her intellect and her love of English literature.'

'So you spend half your days reading poetry to her and discussing obscure nineteenth-century classics. Oh, well,' Yvonne sprang to her feet, 'better you than me! The sea is calling—see you!'

Laurel watched Yvonne snatch up her beach jacket and run from the room. Her half smile was a little wry and not for the first time she found herself envying the younger girl's riding ability.

They had been at the *castillo* for three days and Yvonne was having the time of her life. She adored horses, and immediately the Conde had discovered she was a proficient horsewoman he had provided a suitable mount from his stable and each morning escorted her himself, high on the superb black stallion called Caesar. Yvonne was certainly seeing the island from an undoubted vantage point, and her guide could not be bettered. After the ride came coffee, partaken with

Laurel and the Condesa in the Condesa's apartment, and in the afternoons the two girls swam, sunbathed, and explored the extensive gardens of the *castillo*. The Conde seemed to be setting himself to be the perfect host, nothing was too much trouble for his young guests, and Yvonne revelled openly in the dark, sardonic charm he enfolded her in so effortlessly.

Laurel herself maintained reservations. She was too conscious of her own vulnerability where he was concerned, and also of the guilt still niggling at her every time she remembered the deception she and Yvonne were practising. Yvonne had no qualms, but Laurel's conscience was not so easily appeased by the younger girl's careless reassurances. But it was too late now, she told herself. She'd had the ideal opportunity that first evening. Sighing, she closed the door of her room and made her way downstairs and along to the Condesa's apartment. Somehow she wished the Conde would stop being so utterly charming; if he reverted to his former angry mien towards herself perhaps she would not feel so guilty ... And Mr Searle *had* enjoined secrecy ...

Maria, the Condesa's maid, answered her light tap on the door and bade her to enter. The Condesa was sitting in her high-backed carved chair by the open french doors, her silver-topped ebony cane by her knee, and a polished occasional table piled with antique volumes to the side of her chair. When she saw her visitor a light of warmth glowed in her fine, dark eyes.

The Condesa was eighty years old, and the painfully twisted old hands betrayed her affliction, but despite this she sat erect, her fine head held high, and every line of the chiselled bone structure beneath the still petal-soft skin betrayed the beauty she had once been and the breeding of the aristocrat.

She smiled. 'Welcome, my dear. Come and sit down. Maria, you may leave us for a while.'

Laurel crossed the spacious room and seated herself in the comfortable basket chair opposite the Condesa. A soft breeze drifted across the terrace, bringing the scents of the gardens and the musical drone of the bees on their eternal quest for nectar, and just beyond the columbine-wreathed arbour a graceful fountain plashed its cool, tinkling rain.

'Are you admiring my fountain?' asked the Condesa.

'Yes—all your garden, in fact,' smiled Laurel. 'It's very beautiful.'

'My grandson had it newly—how do you say it?— rescaped—no, landscaped, for me two years ago, when I was forced to admit I could no longer take walks through the grounds. But I still endeavour to take a little stroll in my special domain,' the Condesa added quickly. 'I wonder, will you be patient with an aged woman and lend me your arm, my dear?'

'Yes, of course.' Laurel stood up.

'The air is so fragrant this morning.' The Condesa clasped her hands painfully on her cane, and with Laurel's ready aid rose to her feet.

Slowly the old lady made her way across the terrace and along the broad, even path that meandered among the sculptured shapes of lawn and massed banks of flowers. The Condesa knew each bloom by name and enthused over each especially prized blossom. 'My grandson chose my favourites and ensured that no steps would interrupt the levels so that I might still walk among my beloved flowers. He is a good grandson, do you not agree?'

'I'm sure he is,' Laurel said gently. She turned her head, looking about for the source of the bird song and cries which had begun to fill the air. They did not seem to come from the wild birds that fluttered and twittered under the eaves of the summer house.

The Condesa noticed the questing glance and smiled. 'José is feeding my birds—you will see in a moment, my dear.'

The path was approaching a tall scrolled iron gate set in a high hedge interwoven with a mass of pink, bell-like flowers. Laurel opened the gate and stood aside to allow the Condesa to pass through, then followed. She found herself in a large, circular clearing ringed by shrubs and arbours with seats, and flowering trees. In the centre of the clearing was a huge domed aviary from whence came the noisy orchestra of bird sound and the rainbow flashing of many bright wings. José stood within the enclosure, a satchel on his hip from which he produced handful after handful of seed, and the birds were clustering about him, some alighting on his head and shoulders and others swooping and darting to him, totally unafraid.

Laurel had many reservations about confining birds, and she had heard so many reports of the cruelty inflicted on trapped wild birds in certain continental countries, including the infamous practice of blinding songbirds in the belief that they might sing the better, that she pressed nearer to the mesh to assure herself that no such horror had taken place here. But the Condesa must have perceived something of her fear and touched her arm.

'No, my dear,' she smiled, 'you need have no concern. My feathered creatures are well tended and have no fear of us. See,' she gestured to the leafy branches and shady undergrowth within the aviary, 'everything has been done to provide them with a near natural habitat, and they have ample space for flight. Some of these birds are quite rare, many of them tropical species, but they live and thrive here far more safely and for much longer than they would in their wild forests.'

Laurel could see this, and she relaxed, her interest caught as the Condesa pointed out her favourites, explaining their origins and how they had been carefully selected to eliminate risk of predatory breeds.

'And now,' the Condesa turned with movements which obviously brought pain, but to which her indomitable spirit refused to yield, 'we will sit here for a little while. It is cooler here for you, for that so delicate English complexion of yours, is it not?'

Laurel accompanied her hostess to one of the arbour seats, where it was indeed pleasantly shaded from the hot, strong sunlight. The Condesa chattered desultorily about her garden, but within a few minutes the con-

versation returned to the subject of her grandson, to
whom there could be no doubt of her devotion. Laurel
was shocked to learn that his parents, the Condesa's son
and daughter-in-law, had died tragically in an air
disaster when their son was only sixteen, and within
six months a further cruel blow struck the family when
the Condesa's husband suffered a fatal stroke while
visiting relatives in Madrid.

The Condesa sighed and gave a gesture of resignation
at Laurel's murmur of sympathy. 'What is to be ... I
can say that now, but at the time ... My beloved husband and my only son taken from me in so short a space
of time; my faith was tested to its utmost. But the
burden of responsibility fell heavily on my grandson's
shoulders, before he had even completed his education.
Valderosa, and a household of womenfolk dependent
on him.'

The fine old eyes misted as they looked back in time.
The Condesa had three daughters, two of whom had
since married, and the third, Costenza, of whom the
Conde had already spoken to Laurel, had chosen to remain at Valderosa. 'A rebel, that one.' The Condesa's
lips compressed. 'She wished to make a marriage of
which we disapproved, and so she refused to counten-
ance the suitor we had chosen. Now, I wonder if she
regrets her fine show of independence, when she has
nothing to look forward to but her old age, and a new
mistress in her home when my grandson eventually
marries, as marry he must.'

Poor Costenza, thought Laurel. Just another victim
of the old Grandee tradition of mapping out their
daughters' futures regardless of whether love entered
into it or not. But she kept silent, out of deference to
her hostess and also because of an unexpected flash of
curiosity; had the Conde's bride been chosen? What
was she like? Mental pictures of a sultry-eyed raven-
haired *señorita* or a dark, fiery Andalusian beauty
floated into Laurel's imagination, and suddenly it
became very urgent that she should know ... She
looked eagerly at the Condesa, and saw a smile of

reminiscence hovering on the firm old lips. But it seemed she was to be disappointed.

'I fear Carlota has taken after my foolish daughter. But ah, many times worse! From childhood she has defied authority, and now this latest escapade!' The Condesa paused, momentarily beyond words to describe her opinion of the erring Carlota. She sighed. 'At one time her parents had hopes that perhaps she might grow to be a fitting bride for my grandson, although we had reservations about yet another intermarriage in the family. But Rodrigo has not given any indication that this would meet with his favour. I sometimes think it was perhaps not wise in all ways to allow him to complete his education at your famous old university. Those dreaming spires imbued him with a somewhat broader outlook on life than we expected.'

The Condesa paused, then gave a wry smile. 'And so tomorrow we are to be—how do you say it? Incommoded?—by this troublesome minx, while Rodrigo removes himself well out of reach of her tantrums.'

Laurel hid a smile. She could not imagine Rodrigo being disconcerted by any minx of a girl, no matter how turbulent the tantrums, nor could she imagine him failing to deal summarily with the offender.

'But she is still very young, isn't she?' Laurel murmured. 'It isn't always easy to see life from the viewpoint of someone of another generation.'

The Condesa's chin jerked up annoyedly. 'Carlota will not see life or reason from any viewpoint but her own. As you will no doubt discover for yourself very soon, *señorita*,' the old lady added with a touch of malice.

'I trust not,' Laurel said lightly. 'I have to do something to repay your grandson's kind hospitality.'

'Perhaps,' the Condesa shot her a sidelong glance, 'but I am afraid that Rodrigo will have to deal with the problem himself. As though he did not have sufficient to worry him!'

Laurel felt a flash of amusement. Only a moment ago the Condesa was grumbling because he would not be at home to deal with the recalcitrant Carlota! She smiled. 'I think my sympathy will be needed by Carlota, all the same.'

'Then it will be misplaced,' the old lady said tartly.

Laurel raised her brows.

'It is Carlota's parents who should ensure she responds to discipline, not, ultimately, my grandson. But he is still conscious of the debt he owes to the family, whose combined efforts enabled him to be absent from the island while he completed his education. Now, sometimes, I fear that he takes duty too seriously, to his own detriment.'

'Detriment?'

'Perhaps that is not the word I seek.' The Condesa sighed impatiently. 'No matter, I think you know what I mean when I say he sacrifices much of himself for the family, and for Valderosa and the island.'

'But it is his inheritance,' Laurel said gently.

'True. But an island estate such as this brings grave responsibility. Perhaps to you, *señorita*, our island seems insignificant and our way of life a simple one. But here we are self-supporting, and our economy finely balanced. There are few so-called more advanced countries who can boast of that in today's financial clime. But it does not happen by good luck,' the Condesa said grimly, 'and already our young look to the ways of the outside world, to the trappings and artifices of technology and the spoils of commercialism. For some countries it will work, has become essential to continue to expand, but for our island with its limited resources I fear that too many breaks with tradition could bring disaster.'

The old lady fell silent, then she planted her hands firmly on the top of her cane. 'I talk too much!' she exclaimed. 'And I monopolise too much of your time. Let us return to the house.'

Laurel escorted the Condesa back to the terrace and saw her into the care of Maria. There was no sign of the Conde, but Yvonne had returned from her ride, flushed happily and glowing with health. The two girls spent the rest of the day in leisurely exploration of the *castillo* grounds and a walk to the little port to buy stamps and send off cards to friends. Darkness fell as they reached the *castillo* again and went to their rooms to shower and change for the evening meal.

As always, the dishes were superb, and their host at his most charming. The Condesa was present, and Laurel found her thoughts returning to the confidences made to her that morning in the garden. In the light of this new knowledge she felt forced to revise her impressions of the Conde, and to feel the warmth of understanding springing when she thought of the tragedy fate had brought to him in his youth. Perhaps this responsibility had forced him to be arrogant and unyielding; without that tempering Destino might well have become a poverty-stricken island and the estate a victim of the auction room. But the hands on the reins, if youthful, had not faltered, and nowhere on the island had Laurel glimpsed poverty. There was a bright new school, white and airy and blending perfectly with the old traditional houses, on the hillside above the thriving little seaport, and the new clinic set in beautifully laid-out gardens overlooking the bay, with wide verandas where the white-coifed, serene-faced nursing Sisters could be glimpsed as they tended their patients, although Laurel suspected that there was not an alarming number of these; the people of Destino looked fit and resilient, and the likelihood of long waiting lists for admission was very remote.

Laurel sipped her wine, her eyes reflective as she savoured the velvet richness of the full red wine with its subtle undertone of brandy which along with citrus fruit was the island's chief export. Yes, a great deal of unseen work would be necessary to husband and co-ordinate the resources and skills of the island to their utmost, and who else was there to guide and nurture, other than the Master of Destino? Laurel sighed, unaware that she did so, and suddenly become aware of silence. She turned her head and saw the Conde had risen to his feet.

'You will forgive me, Abuelita ... *señoritas* ...' he inclined his head gravely to each of them in turn, 'I have some dull and tedious paperwork I must complete tonight. Please call on José should you require anything further.'

He moved to his grandmother's side and touched his lips to her frail hand, and with a further courteous nod to Laurel and Yvonne he went from the room.

A strange ennui seemed to descend on the room when the door closed on his tall figure, as though a vital force had also departed. The Condesa uttered an exclamation of despair. 'See? He cannot rest! Always some duty calls. I tell him he needs a bride and many sons to help him. For soon he will become *soltero*, and no *hijos*, and then what will become of Destino? But he will not listen to me!'

Laurel smiled sympathetically. 'I think it will be a long time before your grandson becomes an old bachelor, Doña Luisa.'

'Perhaps,' the Condesa did not sound convinced, 'but time steals past ever more fleetly with each passing year, as even you, *chica*, will discover eventually. And then, one day, one awakes and realises that youth has gone. *Ay! Peinar canas* ...'

The old lady's eyes dimmed with sadness, and Laurel sought for some cheering remark. But to her surprise Yvonne jumped up and ran to the Condesa, putting impulsive young arms round her black-clad shoulders.

'No, you've got it all wrong,' Yvonne cried earnestly. 'It isn't being old in body that matters, it's staying young in heart! Just believe that and you'll never grow old!'

The Condesa looked a trifle surprised, then she smiled and touched Yvonne's cheek. 'Bless you, my child. Perhaps you may be right. I must tell that to my aged and aching bones! But come, let us have some more wine and talk of more cheerful things!'

Certainly there was nothing senile about the Condesa's intellectual qualities. José brought more wine and she regaled the two girls with anecdotes of her youth, her husband, her family, and her childhood home in Castile. An hour flew by, and at last she stopped. 'I talk too much—like all Spanish women!'

The girls escorted her to her suite and the care of Maria, and then wandered back to the *sala*. There were distant voices from the direction of the kitchen quarter, but otherwise the *castillo* was silent. 'I'm going to have a few minutes in the garden—coming?' Laurel asked.

Yvonne shook her head. 'I want to wash my hair— it got so sticky with sea-water this morning. And I'm not going to risk it looking like rats' tails when Carlota arrives.'

Laurel grinned. 'Be honest! It's not Carlota you want to look your best for.'

'I don't know what you mean,' Yvonne said airily. 'Anyway, he's leaving tomorrow, isn't he?'

She scampered off, and Laurel went out into the garden, her face thoughtful. She hoped that Yvonne wasn't going to fall for the magnetic aristocrat of Destino. During the past few days he seemed to have favoured the younger girl particularly, almost as though he had set out deliberately to charm her, taking her riding and swimming and treating her with suave, velvet charm that was guaranteed to turn a head far more stable than Yvonne's. But perhaps she was imagining things. He was simply being a perfect host, and probably trying to ensure that Yvonne had no opportunity for seeking the dangerous attentions of Renaldo.

Laurel wandered through the archway and into the wide courtyard, trying to dismiss the disturbing thought. She should be thankful that everything had worked out so well. Yvonne could have proved a most troublesome handful, and she seemed to have forgotten completely the unsuitable paramour from whose ken her father had had to remove her. In fact, she was turning over a new leaf!

The night air was sweet and heady. The wrought

iron lamps cast a golden glow through which the night
insects fluttered gauzy wings, and the scents of the
garden tempted like will-o'-the-wisps. Laurel passed
under the inky shadows of the *castillo* and quietly
opened the iron-grille door that led into the arboretum.
Here a path wound under the sleeping branches of
flowering shrubs and aromatic pines and sloped down
to a crazy-paved terrace immediately above the sea.
There was a low wall clad with creeper and rock plants,
and here Laurel stood, to gaze out across the moon-
swept bay. Who would have thought a month ago that
she would be here!

She had no idea how long she stood there, just
savouring the cool sweet night and the heavenly vista
spread before her, unable to make the move that would
take her back indoors. The sense of sweet timelessness
was a spell too potent to break. Then, just as she
decided she must tear herself away, she heard the rich,
vibrant notes of a guitar.

Laurel stiffened, her fingers tensing on the rough
stone parapet, then she relaxed, laughing weakly at
herself for her moment of shock. Sound carried a long
way on such clear air; it was probably José or one of
the other servants relaxing before seeking the night's
rest. But it did sound very close ...

She turned, to make her way back the way she had
come, and again froze as a movement in the shadows
caught the corner of her vision.

'Did I startle you, *señorita*?'

The voice came softly, its mocking notes strangely
in harmony with the rippling strum of the guitar, and
very near. She saw the luminous blue-white of a man's
shirt, and the metallic glitter of the instrument, and
then as she moved forward uncertainly a hand shot out
and fastened round her wrist. She was drawn forward,
till she came against hard thighs and looked into the
shadowy features of the Conde.

'You are in a hurry to return?'

'N-no.' She looked at the niche in the terrace, over-
shadowed by the heavy foliage above, and the curved

iron seat. 'I didn't hear you, when I—until you started to play.'

'Perhaps I did not intend you to.' His grasp slackened and slid away, and she stared at him, instantly leaping to a conclusion.

'I'm sorry, I didn't know you were here. I wouldn't have interrupted.'

'You are not interrupting.' He put the instrument aside. 'Please sit down, *señorita*, or courtesy will force me to stand up.'

Uncertainly, Laurel sat down, her back straight and stiff. 'I—I didn't expect to find you here, at this hour, playing. Why didn't you speak, and I'd have gone away and left you in peace, *señor*.'

'Why shouldn't I be here at this hour? And why should I not relax? As for your unwise little query, *señorita*; had I spoken to you out of the darkness I fear you would have suffered fright.' He was very near her. 'Was not the music the most suitable way of betraying my presence?'

'But you said—Oh, never mind.' Laurel looked down at her hands, aware of the fact that she should be making a firmer effort to extricate herself from this unexpected encounter and also that she had a marked reluctance to start making that effort. 'Please, *señor*, continue to play and relax, and let me listen for a while.'

'It is my pleasure, *señorita*.'

He drew the guitar across his knee and began to play.

Laurel listened with increasing pleasure. His musicianship was quite superb, not the idle strumming of a mere accompaniment but the full rich haunting sounds of old Spain, alive with insistent rhythm and the dark warm pulse of passionate flamenco. When the final dramatic notes throbbed into silence Laurel drew an unsteady little breath. At last she murmured, 'I never dreamed you could play like that.'

'You are surprised, *señorita*?'

'You are full of surprises, *señor*!'

There was a brief silence, then, 'But music and dance and art are a living part of our heritage. Why should this surprise you?'

She shook her head, aware of his dark eyes studying her closely. 'I would not have thought you could spare much time for such pursuits.'

'Ah! My grandmother has been talking to you.'

'Yes.' Laurel looked down at her hands, the beginning of an idea occurring suddenly. Impulsively she turned to face him. 'I wonder, *señor* ...'

'Yes?' he prompted.

'You mentioned paperwork tonight. Is there anything I could do to help? While I'm here? I am a secretary, used to dealing with business matters. I thought,' she rushed on, becoming a little self-conscious, 'perhaps I could do some of your letters or invoices ... it would be a kind of return—a very small one—for your hospitality.'

It was so long before he replied that Laurel began to regret her rash offer, then she visibly relaxed as she saw his teeth glint in a smile. 'So this is the reason for your so thoughtful mien this evening at dinner. You are concerned about me?'

She bit her lip, positive that he was laughing at her. 'Well, yes, in a way,' she said with a defiant little movement of her head.

'I am touched, *señorita*, deeply.'

Laurel felt a prickle of irritation. 'Well, as long as you are not angry, *señor*.'

'Angry! Why should I be angry?'

'Don't ask me,' she retorted with spirit, 'but somehow I seem to evoke something remarkably like anger in you, when I least expect it.'

'*Señorita*, you astound me!'

'Perhaps I am progressing, then.'

'Or treading warily?' He stroked his chin with long lean fingers.

Laurel's mouth compressed. 'I have reason for that!'

'Reason!' The long fingers stilled. 'Do I infer from that remark that you are *afraid* of me?'

'Not afraid, *señor*, I object to your method of punishment,' she flashed.

'But offenders do not usually have any choice about their punishment,' he said smoothly.

She knew he remembered, and knew she was venturing back on dangerous ground, but temerity drove her on. 'Not where you are concerned, *señor*, I'm sure. But tell me, do you always punish your women with angry kisses?'

'If they deserve it; yes! I have found it is the only way of silencing them!'

'Oh, you're incorrigible!' Laurel sprang up. 'I think I'd better go—it's late.'

'Before you invoke my anger again?' The needling tone was back in his voice again. '*Señorita*, take care. I am endeavouring to remember our pax, but you are making it extremely difficult for me.'

'Am I?' Her shoulders moved. 'I only intended to offer my assistance.'

'Which I sincerely appreciate,' he stood up, 'but I fear you have forgotten one small but vital consideration.'

'Such as?' She whirled to face him.

'I would not wish to disparage your business qualifications, *señorita*, in your own language.'

For a moment the meaning in his tone eluded her, then suddenly she realised and cursed her stupidity. How could she forget that those letters she would willingly have typed would be couched in a language of which she knew scarcely a word? She gave a rueful exclamation, and tried to laugh.

'I am an idiot! I don't know how I——'

'Forgot?' His features were in deep shadow and she could only guess at the mood in his expression. She made a movement away, and he said quickly, 'Don't go—and please don't say, "It's late" again. I begin to think you must have some possessive person in your life, *señorita*. Someone who has managed to instil a sense of guilt if you are missing for more than an hour.'

Surprise robbed her of response. How had he guessed? She said quietly, 'My parents died when I was a small child and my aunt brought me up. She was kind but very strict, and right up till I left home to work in London two years ago she insisted that I be home before a certain time each night. I have never managed to shake off the habit of worrying about the time once eleven is past.'

'I see. So we both share one sad feature in our lives.' She remembered, and nodded.

'And so now you try to break the bonds of discipline.'

'Not really. I realise now it gave me a kind of strength.' She hesitated, and looked beyond his dark outline to the silver shimmer on the sea. 'You may not believe me, but it took a great deal to persuade myself to—to swim as I did that first afternoon when—when you . . .'

'I have not forgotten! And there is much I begin to understand.' Suddenly his hands closed about her shoulders and tightened as her tremor of surprise communicated itself to him. 'No, *señorita*,' he murmured softly, 'it is not late, and there is no stern guardian with a watchful eye on the clock!'

Laurel trembled. What was to happen was inevitable, yet a force beyond her control rendered her helpless to make even the token protest inhibition urged was necessary. She whispered, 'No—except for yourself, *señor* . . .'

He laughed softly. 'But I am a man, *señorita*, and very human—although I know you are somewhat doubtful about that second respect.' He drew her closer, slowly, until she was enfolded closely in the circle of his arms, her thudding heartbeats meeting a strong, rhythmic response as she was pressed against the hard warmth of him. His mouth hovered above her own for a moment, touched her lips lightly, once, twice, and then took full sweet possession.

She stood immobile within his arms, her own hands wanting to reach round him yet uncertain to make the response, while somewhere in the depths of her solar plexus a fuse began to smoulder. The kiss began to stop, lingered, and then she was taking an unsteady breath. Her lids fluttered open, to reveal that waiting, devastating mouth only an inch away and the blaze of bright stars beyond the outline of his dark head.

He said softly, 'You see, my doubting little *inglesa*, a kiss is not always a punishment!'

Laurel's mouth parted tremulously, and he gave a smothered gasp. '*Por Dios!* Such sweet temptation ...' His arms tightened and his head blotted out the watching stars.

The fuse raced and exploded into a myriad tingling sparks, and Laurel's hands found their way round his shoulders, thrilling to the warm hard whipcord of muscle under the sensuous silk covering of his shirt, wanting to keep and hold for ever and ever ... Aeons or instants later he broke the kiss and pressed her face into his shoulder, while the fire of his lips burned small sweet crosses into the tenderness of her throat and neck, and lingered in the hollow of her shoulder. Then she heard the slight roughness of his indrawn breath. Slowly he released her and took her hands in his, raising them to his lips.

'Perhaps I had better escort you back to sanity, *carina mia!*'

He picked up the guitar and placed his free hand under her elbow. In silence he guided her back to the *castillo*, occasionally checking her where she would have stumbled in the darkness of the arboretum. Laurel's senses were in a whirl and she hardly knew what he said when they were indoors and he halted at the foot of the wide staircase. She looked up at him and saw an unfathomable light smouldering in his dark eyes, and she had to look away lest in the light he should read the truth in her own eyes. Never had she been kissed like that before. Never had she imagined that a kiss could be like that!

'*Buenas noches, señorita,*' he said gravely.

'Goodnight, *señor,*' she whispered—and fled.

CHAPTER SEVEN

LAUREL awakened in a dreamlike state the following morning, half inclined to scoff at herself—she must have imagined that idyllic interlude the previous evening. But she knew it had been no dream; just the memory of it started the tingles chasing up and down her spine. She bathed and dressed and examined her reflection closely in the mirror, sure that large signals would be written all over her to announce to the world that she was in love. But there were no obvious signals, except the secret little half smile that insisted on dancing at the corners of her mouth, and the sharing of a certain wonderment between the bright eyes in the mirror and her own wide-questioning glance.

Suddenly she was dissatisfied with her appearance. She whipped off the blue cotton sleeveless dress she had just donned and turned back to the wardrobe, taking down the new embroidered peasant blouse she had not yet worn and the scarlet dirndl skirt with a swirling frill. The dirndl made her waist look tiny, and the blouse emphasised her small pointed breasts in a way that made her feel excitedly feminine. She brushed her hair again, leaving it flowing loose in a cloud that reached her shoulders, added a touch of perfume and a slick of lip colour, then was impatient to be gone. She couldn't wait to get downstairs to *desayuno* to see . . .

She met Yvonne outside, and scarcely restrained herself from hugging the younger girl in joyous greeting. But Yvonne was not wearing the expression of someone who is in the mood to love the whole world because of loving one special person. To the query, 'Sleep well?' Yvonne shrugged.

'Okay—I usually do. And why are you so cheerful this morning?'

Heavens! Did it show as much as that? Laurel turned

113

to close her bedroom door before she followed Yvonne along the wide gallery. 'Why shouldn't I be cheerful?' she returned lightly.

'Don't ask me—I haven't been at the cream!'

Laurel gulped. 'What's that supposed to mean?'

'Ho ho!' Yvonne giggled. 'You can't see yourself, Laurie.'

For an awful moment Laurel wondered if by some mischance Yvonne had been out last night and witnessed that precious and revealing little interlude. She felt the tell-tale colour rushing into her cheeks as she exclaimed: 'Well, for heaven's sake tell me if I look frightful or something!'

'Something, yes!' Yvonne paused at the top of the staircase and dissolved into further mirth. 'Honestly, Laurie, you're a scream. Of course you don't look frightful—you never do. But this is the first time I've seen you with your hair down and looking all sexy and give-it-to-me-quick instead of a prim old turn-off. That blouse ... wow!'

'Thank you!'

'Well, you know what I mean. Who's it in aid of?'

'Don't be ridiculous!'

'Suit yourself. I say, can I borrow it some time?'

'If you like.' Laurel felt the warmth begin to evaporate from her cheeks with the realisation that she should remember how outspoken Yvonne could be. Then the warmth came back as Yvonne turned and gave her another frankly assessing survey.

'Of course it would look far better without a bra under it.'

'Maybe.' Laurel's mouth tightened. 'But I haven't burned all mine yet, and you just remember what your father said.'

'I've a shocking memory!' Yvonne giggled again, quite unabashed, and danced her fingers down the smooth, mellow old polish of the banister. 'Wish I dare slide down.'

Laurel sighed under her breath, thankful there were some limits to Yvonne's daring. She still felt a twinge of hurt at Yvonne's blunt remark: a prim old turn-off, indeed. Was that really how she appeared to a sixteen-year-old? Did four years' seniority make so much difference?

Yvonne started to sing softly, a snatch of her favourite hit of the moment, then, just as they reached the last few stairs, she broke off to ask abruptly, 'Where did you get to last night? I wanted to borrow your setting lotion, and I couldn't find you anywhere,' she added accusingly, taking the last two stairs in one bound. 'I wondered what on earth had happened to you.'

'And why should anything have happened to Señorita Daneway?'

The Conde stood in the doorway of the *sala*, his stance relaxed but his tone subtly challenging. 'Did you fear some harm had befallen her?' he asked.

Yvonne laughed. 'You never know! She might have been abducted by the phantom of Destino—except that those sort of things don't happen to Laurie!'

Laurel scarcely heard the flippant retort. She was conscious of his gaze moving up to her, and although his dark eyes seemed to study her flushed face she knew he was taking in every line of her as she stood stock-still on the third stair. Under that encompassing scrutiny with no undertones of the warmth she remembered she began to feel uncertain and not a little perturbed. How long had he been standing there? And how much of Yvonne's careless chatter had he overheard?

He held out one hand in a commanding gesture. 'Come, *señoritas—desayuno* awaits.'

Laurel thought she detected a note of impatience, of boredom, almost, beneath the surface Latin courtesy, and suddenly it was as though the enchantment spun the previous evening was a nebulous dream after all. He had reverted again to the cool, arrogant grandee whose mood and reactions she could never predict.

The air of uncertainty seemed to hang over the *castillo* in general that morning. After breakfast the Conde made formal apologies to his two guests, regretting that he must neglect them and entreating them to request anything they wished of José or the other servants. The Condesa kept to her own suite, having her meals served there, and let it be known that she was feeling indisposed that morning. There was much evidence of preparations by the servants for the advent of Carlota, more noise and a great deal of to-ing and fro-ing along the corridors upstairs, and more raised voices from the kitchen quarters. A considerable commotion, in fact, as Yvonne remarked when she and Laurel made their way down to the beach.

'I only hope she's not one of these imperious types, wanting her own way all the time,' Yvonne said darkly. 'If she thinks she can order me about she's got another think coming.'

Laurel smiled wryly. 'That's really why we're here,' she reminded the suspicious Yvonne.

'You mean that's why *you* are here,' retorted Yvonne. 'It's got nothing to do with me. You're the one who's got to keep her in order while His Nibs is away.'

Laurel had not forgotten, and as the afternoon wore on, nearing the time of the steamer's arrival, she felt the return of all her doubts. What if Carlota proved as difficult and headstrong as all accounts of her seemed to indicate? How was she going to deal with her, vested with only the frail authority of a stranger? It was all very well for the Conde to talk of providing companionship and assuming that the presence of two young guests would ensure that Carlota behaved herself as befitted a hostess in her cousin's absence. But once he was gone, what then? What if Carlota decided to remove herself on the next boat? How would Laurel stop her? For there was no one else, except a frail old lady whose advancing years deserved peace and quiet.

Shortly after five the Conde departed, presumably to meet the incoming steamer and his cousin. From the window of her room Laurel saw the tall figure stride out to his car, and even from this distance she could discern the hard set of his features and the air of purposefulness that hung about him, as though he

were prepared for trouble and had every intention of
dealing with it summarily. From the room behind her
there was a chinking sound of glass on glass as Yvonne
pottered among the cosmetics on the dressing table and
knocked over a bottle of nail lacquer.

'Laurie, can I try this mascara tonight—mine seems
to have gone thick?'

'If you like.'

The preoccupied note in her tone brought Yvonne
to the window, in time to see the car move away.
Yvonne's mouth pouted. 'He might have taken us down
to meet her.'

Laurel sighed at the voicing of her own disappointment at this omission, but she gave no hint of it as she
murmured, 'Why should he? After all, he may not want
strangers present at a family meeting.'

'Yes, but we're guests, aren't we? Supposed to be
here for her benefit.' Yvonne turned from the window,
her glance going to the crisp white dress whose hanger
was hooked over the top of the wardrobe door. 'Are you
changing?'

'I think we'd better.' Laurel began to divest herself
of her blouse and skirt. 'I'm beginning to feel somewhat less than fresh.'

'Well, I'm not bothering, not until dinner tonight.
If you want to get dressed up and stick around on your
best behaviour you can.' Yvonne shoved her thumbs
into the top of her jeans and sauntered to the door. 'I'm
going out again.'

'For goodness' sake, don't be long.'

'Depends where I go.'

The door swung shut and Laurel bit her lip. She
knew from her brief weeks of experience of Yvonne's
moods that when the younger girl was piqued she
would not listen to reason. But surely courtesy would
triumph over this display of wilful independence.
Laurel hoped so as she changed into the slim cool
lines of the tailored shirtwaister and slipped her feet
into dainty strapped white sandals. For she and Yvonne
were guests within a limited sense of the word; strange,

and for Laurel at least, somewhat painful circumstances had led to their presence at the *castillo*. In truth, they had had little choice in the matter, and Laurel was not likely to forget this, even if Yvonne preferred to forget it.

Laurel drew her hair back into its accustomed french pleat and studied her reflection for a moment before she picked up her bag. Last night seemed far away now; almost like a dream. Perhaps it had been . . .

The great hall was deserted when she went downstairs. The late sun streamed in vivid gold rays across the polished amber and rose parquet floor, and touched the glowing colours of a huge bowl of scarlet and saffron blossoms which stood on a side table. There were flowers everywhere, on the broad window ledges, on two other side tables, and on a tall pedestal at the foot of the stairs, and everything gleamed from a concerted attack by hand, duster and wax polish, the slightly astringent scent of which still lingered in the air.

After a brief wander outside into the courtyard, then to the side terrace, and a glance over the sloping lawns that surrounded the rest of the *castillo* which showed no sign of Yvonne in the vicinity, Laurel returned indoors. In the small *sala* she settled down with a book to read and wait. But she found it extremely difficult to concentrate on Carlyle's *Critical Essays*, even though the Condesa's extremely comprehensive grasp of his works had shamed her during a discussion the previous day and she had wryly accepted the somewhat triumphant offer of the loan of the old lady's beautiful leather-bound edition of his works. Laurel could recall only the acid observation regarding the intelligence of the population of England once attributed to the literary Mr Carlyle; as an invitation to explore him further it paled rapidly against the lure of the living moment. The print on the page seemed determined to reform itself into a dream picture never intended by the author, one which no doubt Mr Carlyle would have disapproved intensely in a chaste young maiden per-

using his admirable prose. At last Laurel closed the
tome and sighed; it was impossible to fight the
memories of the previous night, even though the
doubts of sanity were trying to instil their chill note
of warning.

So the Conde had kissed her in the moonlight. Why
was she getting so steamed up about a kiss? Looking so
dreamy-eyed that Yvonne had instantly become curious.
She'd be crazy to read anything special into those
heart-taking kisses. Just because he had taken her
breath away by being tender, persuasive, beguiling;
evoking a depth of sweet smouldering desire she had
never realised she possessed. But analysed in cold day-
light what did it mean? It was just the physical thing,
wasn't it? The age-old transient magic that flared like
wildfire when the man-woman chemistry began to
work. But that didn't mean she loved him, not so totally
and utterly that her entire life would hold only half
of its complete potential if it were not spent with
him. She hadn't known him long enough to love him;
to the contrary, he had inspired antagonism in her,
an antipathy fully reciprocated. That first meeting ...
those fierce kisses of anger the night she had dared
to argue ...

Laurel stood up and paced across the *sala*, as though
the exertion might disperse the agitation trembling
through her body. She had to be sensible, not moon
and dream and spin romantic fantasies about a man of
the dangerous calibre of the Master of Destino. She had
thought herself in love with Phil, hadn't she? And she
could think of Phil without a single atom of feeling. If
Phil were to walk into the room at this very moment
she would scarcely want to spare him a glance. Hadn't
she always known that with Phil it had been only
physical attraction and the sop to feminine pride that
he should want her. He had tried so often to arouse
her, to make her want him the same way he wanted her,
and a cold little sense of reluctance had always made her
able to resist.

Laurel stared out of the window, for a moment far

away back in her flat. Perhaps that was the only reason she had kept Phil's interest for so many months. As long as she was unattainable, and he refused to admit defeat ... So wasn't this situation exactly the same? The scented night, the moonlight, and a sudden masculine whim had made the Conde decide to amuse himself with the troublesome girl from England who dared to answer him back. And she had fallen for it. Laurel closed her eyes, aware of the wild agitation beating through her veins. Supposing he had chosen to play on her emotions the way Phil had once done. Supposing he had gone on kissing her, kindling that wild wanton need he had touched in her ... Could she have resisted ...?

Laurel shivered. She was afraid of the answer, and the power she now knew he held over her. She had come to Destino believing her heart hurt by one man, and within the space of days she was in danger of losing it completely to a stranger. In danger? Hadn't she lost it already?

Impatient with herself, she ran impulsively to the door, intending to return to her room and reassure herself that the storm within her showed no trace in the outward grooming she had donned a short time ago. But as she set foot on the first stair she heard voices raised angrily and a rush of light footsteps on the parquet. They stopped abruptly, and Laurel turned her head. The Conde was standing by the outer door, and halfway across the hall stood a young girl, staring at Laurel with tempestuous anger simmering in her dark eyes.

Carlota—for it could be no other—was small and slender and dark, with the vivid colouring, olive skin and vibrant flowing black hair of her race, and the imperious bearing characteristic of her breeding, but there the traditional picture ended. Carlota's hair hung in an untidy tangle about her oval face, her slender form was clad in the uniform of youth, well shrunk and faded denim jeans, a tattered camouflage jacket slung carelessly about her shoulders, and beneath it a skin-

fitting cheesecloth shirt with buttons dragging agape
to reveal all too clearly how little she wore beneath.

'Miss Daneway ...' the Conde's voice came like
splinters of ice through the atmosphere, 'will you leave
us, please, for a moment?'

'Of course.' Laurel felt embarrassment, but as she
moved to obey Carlota darted forward.

'No!' The Spanish girl looked defiantly at her
cousin. 'Why do you wish Miss Daneway to leave us,
Rodrigo? You did not tell me she was a servant!'

He took a step forward, his mouth tightening with
visibly controlled anger. 'I think you know very well.
Do not prevaricate, Carlota.'

'*Si*!' she spat. 'I do know! You are ashamed of me!
You bring me here to this fortress, away from my
friends, to punish me. You are angry about my clothes.
And you insult me by bringing an English girl here to
be my companion while you are away enjoying yourself. A gaoler, you mean! Very well. I wish to look at
her. I wish to see this paragon of English virtue!'

Carlota spun round, her dark eyes flashing and small
fists tight with fury, to stare insolently at Laurel with
undisguised resentment. Laurel recovered from her
shock at this unwarranted attack and her own mouth
tightened. Undaunted by the sudden move the Conde
made towards her, she said quietly: 'I am neither
gaoler nor servant, *señorita*, nor have I ever claimed
to be the other. But I will certainly leave you now—
until the Señor Conde can correct these odd impressions only he can have given you.'

She shot a defiant look at him, and in the moments
of silence that followed her words she brushed past
him and walked quickly across the hall, looking neither
to left nor right, and let herself out by the garden door.

When she reached the terrace she was quivering with
pent-up anger. She had been prepared to find Carlota
something of a handful, a rebellious teenager, striving,
like Yvonne, to break free of parental discipline and the
old conventional restrictions whose ghosts were not yet
entirely laid, but she had not expected to meet such

outright dislike so openly expressed. Plainly the young
Spanish girl was possessed of a strong will and a temper
that more than matched, but surely ... Laurel's mind
closed on the temptation to define Carlota's manners
as she tried to calm her natural feeling of hurt. Where
the devil had Yvonne taken herself off to? She was not
exactly an ideal ally, but her presence might at least
have evoked a little more restraint in Carlota.

Laurel reached the fountain and paused, her face
troubled. She held out her hand and let the golden
rain pour its coolness through her fingers. The rich,
deepening sun cast a warm glow on the ancient stone
and heightened the vivid hues of the blossoms, but
Laurel was scarcely conscious of her surroundings.
Carlota's scornful words still stung. *A paragon of
English virtue!*

The echoes evoked an instant picture of a prim,
colourless Victorian miss, rigid in outlook, staid in
manner and smugly correct to the point of nausea.
Laurel did not pause to consider that her definition
might have been considered grossly unfair by many a
radical Victorian miss who seethed under the yoke of
very real restrictions, she was conscious only that her
anger had veered from Carlota to another direction.
What *had* the Conde said to his young cousin? Was
that how he saw——?

'You are angry, *señorita*?'

The crisp, enquiring voice made Laurel's head jerk
round. He was standing quite close to her, his features
darkly shadowed against the sun, so that she could
only guess at the true expression in his eyes. She looked
away from that dark, enigmatic silhouette. 'Have I
not cause?' she parried dryly.

'Do you always return question to question?'

'Yes—if it's the obvious answer.'

'You *are* angry.'

This time it was clearly a statement, and she stayed
silent, her head averted obstinately from the tall figure
and her gaze set unblinkingly on the rainbow glistens
in the spray.

'I am afraid my cousin was unpardonably rude a few moments ago.' His tones were smooth, unemotionally suave. 'May I offer my deepest apologies on her behalf?'

'Thank you.'

There was a silence. Laurel knew that her response could have sounded ungracious, but the smart of anger had turned to hurt and she had an absurd fear that if she looked at him and read amusement in his expression she would dissolve into tears. Oh, she was crazy! Why was she standing here like a foolish child in the sulks? She said in a choked little voice, 'Forget it, Señor Conde ...' and turned away. But instantly his hand closed on her arm, very firmly.

'Laurel ...'

'Well?'

'Surely you are not upset by the thoughtless discourtesy of a wayward child?'

'I would not term Carlota exactly a child,' Laurel retorted stiffly.

'Perhaps not. But I should have thought that your experience of your own charge would have prepared you for the temperamental caprices of an adolescent girl who has, perhaps, been a little too indulged for her own good.'

He paused for a moment, and she took a deep breath, increasingly aware of that lean firm hand curved round her forearm and his masculine presence so disturbingly close. Then he moved, drawing her insistently to face him and raising his other hand to cup the curve of her cheek. Inexorably he turned her head.

'Come, look at me, *señorita*,' he wheedled in soft, bantering tones from which amusement was not far distant. 'Surely it is not *my* fault!'

'But I think it is!' She jerked her head away from that disturbing caress. 'What did you say to her to give her such a—such a scornful impression of me?'

His brows drew together and his dark eyes looked down searchingly into her flushed face. 'But I do not understand.'

'Don't you?'

'No, my indignant little *señorita*, I do not.' The shake of his dark head expressed puzzlement. 'I said nothing derogatory whatsover to cause my cousin to form an opinion of you unfavourable in any way.'

'Well, you succeeded in spite of whatever it was,' she said bitterly.

'So it seems.' The familiar sparks of devilry glinted in his eyes. 'You found Carlota's description unflattering?'

Laurel's mouth tightened. 'I find it ridiculous, *señor*. I can only surmise that for some reason best known to yourself you were endeavouring to set me up as an example. Well, you certainly failed.' She tugged out of his grasp. 'Now please let me go and —*oh!*'

With a completely unexpected movement he had seized her round her waist, and the world tilted wildly as he lifted her high into the air and then sat her firmly on the broad stone rim of the fountain bowl. His laughing, mocking features were now only a little above her eye level and he merely shook his head as she cried out with indignation and shock.

'No, I will not put you down! I have only this moment put you there. Now let us resolve this strange little misunderstanding. Rest assured, *señorita*, that particular choice of words was not mine. I can only suggest that Carlota's grasp of English is not quite as accomplished as we have always believed. I wonder,' his teeth glinted in a brief smile, 'if inadvertently I did err in my attempts to convey your true character. Shall we define . . . ?'

Laurel struggled. His hands were still clamped tightly around her waist and her knees could not escape the hard thighs braced against them. The falling spray of the fountain behind her sounded unnaturally loud and she could only think wildly of what the Condesa might think if she should chance to look from her window or walk out on her terrace and see the undignified little scene. 'Please . . . let me——!' Another cry escaped her as he suddenly let go and she lost her balance, almost tumbling back into the fountain bowl.

She reached out wildly at the same moment as he relented and caught her again, and she found she was clinging frantically to him, her arms round his neck.

Again he lifted her, laughing openly now, and slowly slid her down within the circle of his arms, holding her imprisoned so that her toes scarcely reached the ground.

'I wonder ...' he said softly, 'a paragon of English virtues. Are you, my *chiquita*? I hope not.'

'You hope not! What do you mean?'

'Paragons are cold goddesses, without the fire of the spirit to warm a man's veins and excite his senses. No, I would not wish you to be that kind of paragon, *señorita*.'

Laurel tried to convince herself that she had not really heard those words, and to keep her cheek away from the sensuous contact with sleek cream silk shirt and the hard male warmth beneath it. She said weakly, '*Señor*, please be serious ... We—we were talking about Carlota.'

'Were we?'

'Yes—it was a mistake—if you've given her the impression that I am here to be a sort of companion with authority,' she murmured feverishly, 'perhaps even spying on her. It's only natural that she will resent me, even hate me. I would feel exactly the same.'

'Would you?' His arms slackened and his hands moved lingeringly down to the small of her back. 'You are trembling, *señorita*. You are not afraid of my temperamental cousin?'

'No, of course not.' Laurel avoided his dark, discerning gaze, well aware that the tremors running through her body were certainly not induced by fear of Carlota. 'It's just that I——'

'The spray has caught you. My foolish—how do you say it?—horseplay?—has caused you distress. Your dress is quite damp.'

It was also somewhat disarranged. Laurel tugged it down as he released her, and felt the colour flow into her cheeks as she realised two of the buttons had come

undone. Her fingers felt clumsy as they tried to discipline the silky material, and awareness of his rather
pointed turning away did not make their task any
easier.

'I should not concern yourself too much with Carlota's tantrums, *señorita*,' he said at last, his features
grave and controlled now. 'My grandmother is, alas,
frail, but Carlota is still a little afraid of her. Come,
we will return, and I think we will find a more civilised
young lady awaiting us.'

He touched Laurel's arm and she looked up en-
quiringly.

His mouth curved sardonically. 'I sent her to her
room with instructions to dress herself more fittingly
before paying her respects to her grandmother.'

The sun had gone now to its bed of crimson glory
and the violet shadows of the evening were deepening
across the garden and touching the old stone walls of
the *castillo* with long fingers of indigo. Already the
night blossoms were giving out their scents and the
promise of yet another perfect sub-tropical evening
lingered on the still air with its subtle invitation to the
senses. But Laurel was anxious only to get indoors to
sanity. She was still shaken from the interlude by the
fountain, even as cool common sense told her that the
Conde had once more chosen to amuse himself with
the English *señorita* whose path had crossed his somewhat disastrously—disastrously for her!—on two occasions already, and she could not shake off a feeling of
premonition that further disaster and Carlota were in-
extricably linked in the future.

The Conde's long, leisurely strides halted as the
path widened and the steps to the terrace glimmered
ahead. Laurel also stopped and looked at him with
unhidden anxiety in her eyes. 'You leave tomorrow?'

He inclined his head.

'You will be away for long?'

'No. One week, perhaps two. Not more. I must return
before our annual *romería*.'

'Is that a festival—special to the island?'

'It is a pilgrimage as well as festival, and yes, it is very special to Destino.' The Conde paused, one hand resting on the stone balustrade, and looked into Laurel's enquiring gaze. 'It is our commemoration of the Little Virgin of Destino—*Nuestra Señora de la Fuente*—you have not yet visited our shrine?'

Laurel shook her head. 'No—is it far from here?'

'A mere seven *kilómetros* or so. It is quite a climb, perhaps, but in the fervour of the occasion one does not seem to notice it. Each year, on the twentieth of May, we make our pilgrimage in honour of the day when our eternal fount was given miraculously to the island in a time of great drought, when our young tender crops shrivelled in a harsh sun and our cattle perished for lack of water. On that day long ago our priest led the islanders in a day and night of special prayer to Our Lady, and our prayers were granted. In a tiny cave Our Lady brought a spring of pure crystal water from the arid rock, and since then it has never been known to dry up all down through our recorded history.'

His voice had softened, losing its normal ring of authority, and Laurel felt strangely moved. She knew that there were many similar legends which were similarly celebrated, but it was none the less moving when one was actually present at the source.

The Conde went on: 'So each year, after special Mass, we make our pilgrimage to the hills and the *ermita* by the shrine. There we give thanks, and afterwards we feast and celebrate in the grounds of the *castillo*. Ah,' he smiled down at her, 'it is a great occasion. I am happy that you will be with us.'

'Thank you, *señor*. I shall look forward to it,' Laurel responded gravely, then obeyed his light touch and began to ascend the steps to the terrace.

In silence they entered the *castillo*, the Conde with that slight smile of good humour playing about his handsome mouth again, but Laurel felt unaccountably depressed. Her earlier anger at Carlota's unfriendly attack had long since vanished, and so had the wild feeling of elation evoked by the little interlude by the fountain—he could evoke happiness in her so easily, she reflected wryly. But even the thought of the *romería* to look forward to could not banish this air of foreboding that had settled like a pall on her spirit. Suddenly the Conde's time of absence seemed to stretch ahead endlessly, bleak and empty, a germinating period ... For what?

Laurel tried desperately to shake off the dull weight of depression, telling herself she was being foolish. She had no concrete reason for fear, had she? There was no real reason why Carlota, or anyone else for that matter, should wish her harm. So why this depression?

She forced a smile as she went to greet the Condesa, who waited for them in the big *sala*, with a now quiet and gracious Carlota—almost demure in a beautiful, high-necked, simply cut white dress—at her side. Yvonne had also returned, and she too looked unusually sedate and on her best behaviour.

The Conde poured wine, and the talk was light and cordial. But still Laurel wished with all her heart that he was not going away ...

CHAPTER EIGHT

THE Conde departed immediately after breakfast the following morning.

Laurel watched him go and wished she didn't feel as though he were taking part of her with him. She had not slept very well, and it was useless to deny to herself the truth of the reason why; by the time he returned to Destino it would almost be time for her to leave. There would be the *romería*, and then only another week remaining before the day provisionally fixed for the return home of herself and Yvonne. Just this moment, seeing his tall figure in cream pants and dark brown shirt, casual suede jacket slung carelessly over his shoulder, get into the car and raise his hand in farewell salute, gave her a heart-shaking pang of loss. Just a forewarning of the emptiness of the days ahead —and all the rest of the days when he and his island were only memories.

She swallowed hard. There had also been the persistent nag of her conscience during the long wakeful hours. The nag that told her she was still shirking an unpleasant task; that of telling him the truth behind her presence on Destino. At first she had felt it was right that her loyalty and sympathy should be on the side of her employer and Yvonne, and Yvonne's own entreaties had been totally genuine. But now ... she desperately wanted to place herself on an honest footing as far as the Conde was concerned—the sense of deceit was unbearable, she felt like a spy!—yet she dreaded what his reaction might be. All this painful division of loyalties had kept her awake and still she had not found her answer. How to tell him and convince him that she had never intended a deliberate deception, and make him understand how the circumstances of her arrival at the *castillo* had been beyond her control. But would he understand? She remembered his anger, the arrogance of his unassailable strength, and her heart quailed. Soon it would be too late. Wouldn't it be better and easier to stay silent? In a short while it would all be over, and the likelihood of ever meeting him again in the more nebulous future was extremely remote. The very thought started the miserable black ache again . . .

'Miss Daneway . . .?'

The attractively accented voice at her shoulder made her start. She turned to meet the wide, direct gaze of Carlota.

The Spanish girl flashed a brilliant smile. 'Or may I address you as Laurel?'

'Of course.' Laurel forced a smile, still wary of the unknown quantity of the Conde's young cousin. 'Please do—Carlota.'

'Thank you.' Carlota hesitated, then bit her lip with apparent ruefulness. 'I should have said last night . . . Will you accept my apologies for my so bad manners yesterday? But I was so angry—I did not realise what I was saying. You will forgive me, *si*?'

Laurel was instantly disarmed. It was difficult to believe that this charming, attractive girl and the tempestuous spitfire of yesterday were one and the same. 'Yes, of course!' She smiled warmly, thankful and relieved that a friendly footing should be established when she had expected sulks and cold unfriendliness.

'Good. And now perhaps——'

'Laurie——' Yvonne bounded down the stairs, 'we're going swimming now. Carlota's going to show me a special little cove—we're going to ride there. Okay?'

Before Laurel could reply the Spanish girl broke in: 'But perhaps Laurel will accompany us?'

'She doesn't ride—and she has a date every morning with your grandmother,' Yvonne said carelessly. 'Are you ready?'

'In a moment. I must tell Abuelita.'

'I think she's going to be fun,' Yvonne remarked when Carlota had vanished in the direction of the

Condesa's suite. 'D'you know, she's six months older than me. But I think I look a bit older—of course I'm taller. Don't you think so?'

Laurel tried to hide amusement, knowing how much Yvonne yearned to be twenty and worldly. 'It depends —on how grown-up a mood *she* happens to be in and how grown-down a mood *you* happen to be in at the same time.'

'Oh, you're mean!' Yvonne pouted, but she was too excited to take umbrage.

A little while later the two girls set off. They had changed into jeans and shirts, long hair flowing and their laughter ringing out across the courtyard of the *castillo* as the groom brought out the horses.

The Condesa had walked stiffly into the main hall, and there was a wistful look in her fine old eyes as she leaned on her silver-topped cane and watched the girls urge their mounts into a trot through the high archway of the *castillo* and out into the open country beyond.

'They speak the same new language, the language of youth which knows no frontiers,' the Condesa observed with a sigh. 'Ah, it is so different today.' She turned and began to make her way back to her world, now made small with the confines of infirmity, leaning slightly on Laurel's arm. When she reached the sunlit patio outside her sitting room she sank painfully into her high chair and gave Laurel a wry glance.

'You should be with them, child, not wasting the sunlit hours pandering to the whims of an infirm old woman.'

'I can't ride—and I don't consider one hour in the morning a waste. It's little enough return for your kindness in making us so welcome,' Laurel said firmly.

The Condesa dismissed this with a wave of her hand. 'No, my dear. I am well aware that my grandson's motive in bringing you here was somewhat less than altruistic. At least he did not make a secret of it—or so he assures me.'

The Condesa sounded tired, and as though she did

not entirely approve of her grandson's arrangements. Laurel's own guilt surfaced instantly and she said quickly: 'No, Doña Luisa. It is I who have cause to be grateful to your grandson.'

'Really?' A sparkle of curiosity lit the Condesa's eyes and she turned her head. 'That sounded quite fervent, my dear.'

Had the Conde not told his grandmother of that fervent-sounding reason? It seemed not, Laurel thought with relief and a flood of warm affection that he had kept her somewhat embarrassing secrets! Aware of the Condesa waiting, she said slowly, 'Yes, Doña Luisa— he helped me out of a very awkward situation, a few days after we had arrived here. For that I shall always be grateful.'

There was a pause, then the Condesa smiled. 'It is a painful memory, and you do not wish to relive it at this moment? I understand, my dear. Certainly I am grateful that your appreciation has taken this form. I do not think I could have maintained my patience with Carlota during my grandson's absence. She is a dear child really, but oh, so exhausting! She would have been bored and resentful if left to amuse herself, but now the problem is solved. I do hope they become good friends ...'

The Condesa's hope was certainly realised during the next few days. Yvonne and Carlota became almost inseparable, riding, swimming, playing together, sharing confidences and developing a close, intense camaraderie that shut out Laurel completely.

She tried not to mind the secrecy of their conversations, which would either cease or mute to whispers and giggles as soon as she appeared, and supposed she should be thankful that she was left with plenty of free time to complete her own research for Mr Searle.

Her folder was becoming quite bulky now, and she decided it was time to begin sketching a new map of the island, adding a code of symbols of her own as a key to her notes. It seemed the best way to collate all the random jottings and make it easier to recall everything clearly when she got home and set it all out for Mr Searle.

She had also taken quite a lot of colour film, which would not be processed until she returned, and she was becoming confident that she was compiling as comprehensive a picture of Destino's potential as she could with her novice's knowledge. Not for the first time she wished she could draw more skilfully and possessed more technical ability to assess what she saw. Those water towers, for instance. There were three of them, stepped up the hillside not far from where she sat, walls dazzling white in the bright sun. She knew that their function was to catch and pump up the water from the little hillside rivulets, but what their capacity might be she had no means of knowing. And the one person who could tell her she dared not ask ...

What would be his reaction? Laurel bit her lip and stared across the peaceful vista with troubled eyes. If only Mr Searle had not bound her to secrecy for the time being! After all, it was only a preliminary survey, and if, as she suspected, water was indeed a precious commodity on the island her boss's hopes might well be dashed for that reason alone, apart from any other. So it was not yet time to begin delicate probes, to sound out the possibility of co-operation from the Master of Destino.

If only she had not met him and become his guest. It wouldn't seem so underhand ... Laurel shook her head. No, she didn't wish that! Why couldn't she be honest? He was the most wonderful, exciting man she had ever met in her entire life. Just to think of him started shivers down her spine, and just to think of his opinion of her if he learned the true purpose of her visit made shivers of another kind possess her body.

Suddenly she made up her mind. She would tell him, the very first opportunity she had after his return. She must. Because if Mr Searle did decide to come out himself to discuss the possibility of opening a holiday centre on the island the Conde would have to know, and he would be so angry at the part she had played that he would probably refuse to begin negotiations at all. It was only logical to reason it out this way, and Mr Searle would be the first to understand.

She felt happier, as though a weight had lifted off her mind with this decision, even though she knew she would be scared when the moment of truth arrived. She gathered up her notes, added a question mark to the water towers, and stood up. Although the island was ideal for activity holidays, for riding, walking, swimming, fishing, and climbing, with scenic views to delight an artist's heart, she could not help hoping secretly that her boss's plan might come to naught. Destino should be left unspoilt and undiscovered. She could not bear the thought of attractive women and provocative girls coming to Destino, perhaps making their way to the Conde's beach as she herself had done, perhaps meeting him, perhaps ...

Yvonne and Carlota overtook her as she made her way back to the *castillo*. They slowed their mounts and looked down at her.

'You enjoy walking, Laurel?' the Spanish girl asked.

'Very much.' Laurel shaded her eyes against the sun's glare as she looked up. 'Have you had a nice morning?'

'Yes, thank you.' Carlota's smile held a tinge of superiority. 'It is a pity you do not ride—you are missing so much, Laurel.'

'Am I?' Laurel was aware of being made to feel wanting in accomplishments and tried to suppress a flash of resentment. After all, she could swim, dance, play a passable game of tennis, read a music score, and she also worked for her living; there were limits to the accomplishments one could fit into one's spare time.

Yvonne giggled. 'Oh, Laurie's experienced this top-of-the-world feeling all right—she has been up on Caesar, you know.'

'On Caesar?' Carlota reined to a halt. 'You have ridden my cousin's stallion? I do not believe it!'

'Oh, he was on as well!' Yvonne giggled.

Laurel flung a furious glance at Yvonne, and the

giggle died from the younger girl's face. 'Sorry, didn't mean to give your secret away, Laurie. It—it was only a sort of joke, Carlota—Laurel couldn't ride Caesar if you gave her a million pounds!'

Carlota's small, imperious features became cold. 'I do not understand the joke.'

'No, does it matter?' Yvonne looked uncomfortably at Laurel and then exclaimed, 'Oh, come on—we'll be here all day if we wait for Laurie.' She dug her heels into the mare's flanks and cantered away. After another cold, suspicious glance at Laurel's set face, Carlota followed.

She was noticeably cool towards Laurel during the midday meal when Laurel returned, but the presence of the Condesa prevented any further probings of an embarrassing nature from Carlota. As soon as the meal was over the two girls excused themselves and Laurel did not see them again until the evening.

She noticed their occasional exchange of surreptitious glances, and wondered uneasily what they were planning. She was not surprised when Yvonne came along to her room as she was getting ready for bed and hung round the dressing table, dipping experimentally into Laurel's jar of moisturiser.

'Can I try it?'

'Help yourself.' Laurel wound her watch and placed it on the bedside table. 'Are you out of it?'

'No ...' Yvonne examined her complexion intently and slowly stroked the fluffy cream into her skin. When she had finished she looked at Laurel through the mirror. 'Laurie ...'

'Yes.'

'Could you let me have some money?'

Laurel stared. 'Are you broke again?'

'Well, not exactly—but I bought a new straw sun hat down in the town today and we had three of those almond *helados* at the café.'

Laurel frowned. 'But your father gave you a hundred pounds for pocket money. You can't have gone through it already. Not here! We've only been in the café two or three times—when *I* paid, incidentally—and you haven't bought anything. Heavens, Yvonne, there are only a handful of shops on the island.'

'I've sent a lot of postcards off, and you know how money dribbles away on odds and ends when you're on holiday.' Yvonne turned round and pulled a face. 'Oh, don't look so shocked. I haven't spent the lot, but Carlota wants to go on a trip tomorrow and I want to be sure I've got plenty of bread.'

'Trip?' Laurel paused in the act of slipping into bed. 'What trip?'

'On the steamer tomorrow.'

'But where?'

'Oh, Laurie, don't fuss!' Yvonne plonked herself down on the edge of the bed. 'We're bored—there's nothing to do here. Carlota knows her way around.'

'Yes, I can imagine that.' Laurie's brow betrayed worry. 'But is she allowed to—to go off wherever she wants? Does the Condesa know?'

Yvonne shrugged. 'I expect so. But we're going—it'll be fun. It must be—we're going to the Happy Isles!'

Dismay widened Laurel's eyes. 'But you can't do that in a day! It took us five hours from Las Palmas. You'll——'

'I know—that's why I must have some extra money. Because we might have to stay overnight. Carlota has some friends there and we'll probably stay with them, but just in case they're away or can't put us up we have to be prepared to stay overnight at an hotel. And I can't let her whack out for me, can I? Oh, come on, Laurie, don't be so stuffy,' Yvonne wheedled. 'It'll be okay, honestly. You know that Daddy gave you the travellers' cheques to look after. You wouldn't want me to have to cable him for more money, would you?'

Laurel took a deep breath. Yvonne's unexpected request had put her in a quandary. A warning instinct made her reluctant to agree, yet did she have any valid reasons for withholding consent? And if she did, would the two girls obey? Laurel had an uncomfortable sus-

picion that they had made up their minds and nothing
either she or the Condesa said would make a scrap of
difference. And what would the Conde say when he
returned? For he would find out. The girls' absence
couldn't be kept a secret; someone, perhaps the Condesa, perhaps even a member of the staff, might mention it quite innocently. Laurel's mouth set.

'No,' she said firmly. 'You must persuade Carlota to
forget this trip, at least until the Conde returns. Then
you can go, if he gives his permission.'

'Laurie! You wouldn't tell him! That's the
whole——' Yvonne stopped, and her features tightened
mutinously. 'I might have known you'd be a spoilsport.
Now you've ruined everything.'

'No, I might just have saved Carlota from a load of
trouble. Now go to bed and forget about it,' Laurel
said shortly.

For a moment it seemed as though Yvonne was about
to fly into one of her tantrums, then she stood up in-
dignantly. 'I might have known you'd come down
heavily with the establishment. You should have been
born a century ago. You'd have fitted in then,' she
added viciously as she flounced out of the room.

It was a long time before Laurel settled into sleep.
Yvonne's angry thrusts had hurt deeply. Was it true?
she asked herself. Was she a spoilsport, and all the
other unflattering things Yvonne and Carlota had
called her with the bluntness of adolescence? Had she
been unreasonable to forbid the trip? But was it so
unreasonable to endeavour to be a responsible member
of society and to have consideration for her host's
wishes—to say nothing of the responsibility entrusted
to her by her employer? Perhaps the trip was just an
innocent escapade, but was it wise to encourage two
youngsters both of whom were at present in bad grace
with their respective families, to flout authority?

At last Laurel fell asleep, beginning to wish bitterly
that Yvonne and Carlota were far enough . . .

The little maid had to call her three times in the

morning before she surfaced from a too late sleep. With
dismay she saw that it was long after eight-thirty. The
maid looked distressed.

'*Lo siento*—I think you wish long sleep today,' she
stammered in her halting English mixed with her own
tongue. '*Lamento este——*'

'No, please don't worry.' Laurel smiled at her. 'It's
my own fault for sleeping so late.'

'*Si*—but *no fue culpa mía*. The *señorita* understand?'
There seemed much the maid wanted to explain, but
she could only grope for what she wanted to say.

Laurel's grasp of Spanish was no better, and she
smiled again, trying to reassure the troubled girl, and
poor Sofía went at last, still shaking her head and
lamenting.

Breakfast was a solitary affair for Laurel that morning, guiltily conscious that everyone else in the household had finished theirs long since and her own tardi-
ness was holding back the staff from getting cleared
away. The girls must have gone riding again, she
thought, hoping Yvonne had got over her sulks. She
finished her coffee and slipped up to her room to wash
her hands and collect her white cardigan in case the
Condesa wished to go out this morning. Judging by the
tossing heads of the flowers in the window boxes outside the breakfast room there was a very strong wind
blowing.

There was no suspicion in Laurel's mind as she
pulled open her dressing table drawer to drop one or
two oddments into it, but she frowned as she looked
down. Surely she hadn't left it so untidy ... Then she
saw the jumbled mix-up of silk headsquares she knew
she had left folded neatly and gave an exclamation of
dismay. The little plastic folder in which she kept their
passports and money was still there, but open, and
several of the travellers' cheques were missing.

Laurel turned pale. She checked them again, and
searched the drawer, and knew there was no mistake.
Yvonne must have crept into the room early that morning and taken what she wanted. A quick look into the

girl's room confirmed her suspicion. Yvonne's smaller case was not there, and quite a few of her clothes and personal belongings were also gone.

Her face set with anger, Laurel returned downstairs, to be met in the hall by Maria with a summons from the Condesa.

Laurel's heart sank. The Condesa had discovered the flight of the two truants and she was to be called to the reckoning. But the Condesa greeted her with her normal graciousness, and bade Maria to leave. Laurel sat down, preparing to break the news, and the Condesa gave her a searching look.

'You seem worried, my child. Is something wrong?'

Laurel swallowed hard and told her.

'*Madre mía!*' The Condesa raised her eyes heavenwards, then closed them for a moment. 'You are certain?'

Laurel nodded unhappily. 'If only I hadn't fallen asleep!' She bit her lip, another suspicion occurring. It was highly probable that Yvonne had carefully instructed the maid to delay the morning call on the pretext that Laurel wanted to sleep late, and poor Sofia had naturally obeyed.

'That troublesome *niña!*' the old lady exclaimed with a thump of her cane. 'She must have commandeered the car and José very early this morning —that boat sails shortly after dawn.'

'He wouldn't question her?'

'José?' the Condesa snapped with unconscious arrogance. 'Indeed not. José is a servant, a very well trained servant. He would not question an order from anyone of our family, or a guest.'

'No, I suppose not,' Laurel said unhappily. 'I hope they'll be all right—I feel responsible.'

Unexpectedly the Condesa gave a wry smile. 'Nonsense! You could not do more than forbid the escapade. After all, one can not forcibly imprison two very determined young girls who have made up their minds on a course of action.'

'Yes, but I'm afraid of what——'

'Of what my grandson will say?'

'Yes.'

'It is quite simple—we will not tell him. Provided they return safely without a tale of trouble! All the same,' the Condesa paused, worry entering her dark eyes, 'we must hope he does not hasten back too quickly.'

Laurel gave an unguarded exclamation. 'He's coming back *today*?'

'Today?' It was the Condesa's turn to look startled. 'I trust not—if we are to keep the little secret. It is to be hoped that he remains away another week.'

'A week!' Laurel stared. 'But the girls should be back by tomorrow evening. It's only a——' She stopped, for the Condesa was shaking her head.

'My dear, I'm afraid they have misled you. The steamer on which they sailed this morning does not go to Las Palmas. It is the weekly service to Madeira.'

'Madeira!'

'Yes.' The Condesa placed both hands over the top of her cane and regarded Laurel with something like satisfaction at the shock she had evoked. 'You may not have realised that although we are quite fortunate in having a number of steamers call here only one of them links us with Madeira, and the return boat is not due for another five days.'

Laurel paled. 'But Yvonne never even mentioned ...' She stopped, unwilling to believe that Yvonne had told her a deliberate untruth.

But as the days passed, with no sign of the truants, she was forced to accept, with increasing worry, the unpalatable fact. Her imagination supplied plenty of varieties of mischief and trouble into which Yvonne, abetted and aided by the equally headstrong Carlota, could plunge, and she suspected that the Condesa, of all people, harboured a secret sympathy for the two girls.

One morning later that week she said rather abruptly: 'You are worried, my dear, are you not?' and when Laurel nodded the Condesa smiled.

'You take responsibility very much to heart, I'm

afraid. Take care you do not miss out on your own youth.'

Laurel stared, and the old lady shook her head, a strangely misted look in her eyes. 'When one is as old as I am, my dear, one begins to see things in a different way. When I was young we were trained very strictly, we had to conform, and because of that we in our turn passed on that legacy of discipline. But today our young are able to reason for themselves and question whether a tradition is the only way, simply because it is a tradition. And I think perhaps some of us who are old are simply envious, because the right to think and decide for oneself was not ours.'

It was all very well for the Condesa to philosophise, Laurel thought with a flash of rebellion; she would not suffer in the row which might erupt. For if the Conde arrived home first and discovered his cousin's wilful absence it was more than likely that he would not display the same liberal views to which his grandmother had suddenly admitted, to say nothing of what Yvonne's father would say if the escapade should come to his ears.

But it seemed that Laurel's misgivings were groundless. The Conde did not return, and the following Thursday evening brought Carlota and Yvonne, looking only slightly timorous of what their reception might be and their suppressed high spirits bubbling over the moment they realised that Laurel was too thankful to see them to be genuinely angry.

'We've had an absolute rave of a time—sorry we sneaked off like that, but it was the only way without a great fuss.' Yvonne gave Laurel an exuberant hug. 'You're not really mad, are you? Look, we've brought you a peace offering!'

'And something for Abuelita,' broke in Carlota. 'Some of your favourite Bual,' she added winningly, kissing her grandmother's cheek as she proffered the bottle of wine.

They had brought an attractive tapestry shoulder bag for Laurel, and although Yvonne's secret little grin at

Carlota did confirm the sad suspicion that the gift was
something of a bribe Laurel had to forgive them.

Carlota seemed to have forgotten her previous ani-
mosity towards Laurel and the meal that evening was
a pleasant occasion. The Condesa joined them and
listened eagerly to the girls' account of their visit.

'I have a dear friend in Funchal,' she said musingly.
'You remember, Carlota? Senhora Pereira—her husband was the Portuguese attaché until he retired and
they bought their villa in Funchal. It is a pity you did
not think to call on her. I have not seen her for such
a long time.'

'But I do remember the Senhora Pereira. Alas, I
could not recall her address, and there are so many
of the name of Pereira,' Carlota said glibly. 'I know!
We will return there immediately! And we will take
you with us, Abuelita!'

'*Madre mía!*' The Condesa cast a despairing glance
heavenwards. 'Whatever next, foolish *niña?*' she exclaimed affectionately. 'I fear I——'

But whatever the Condesa feared was not to be
voiced. José had entered on soundless tread, to hover by
her chair and bend to deliver a message in low tones.
There were moments of silence from the others, then
the Condesa looked at Laurel, something between
puzzlement and amusement in her dark eyes.

'You are required to take a telephone call, my dear.
Well, go, child!' she added sharply as Laurel stared at
her with surprise.

'Yes, but I——' Aware of the others staring at her,
Laurel stood up and remembered to make a murmured
'Excuse me,' to the Condesa as she hurried in the wake
of José. Could it be Yvonne's father calling? Had
something happened ...? The manservant opened the
door of the Conde's study, indicating the gilt and onyx
telephone that stood on a fine old tulipwood *bureau-
plat* by the window and then closing the door noise-
lessly behind her. Laurel picked up the unfamiliar
feeling receiver and said uncertainly, 'Hello, this is
Laurel ...'

There was a soft but distinct chuckle at the other end, and a deep voice with a note of mockery responded, 'Please do not sound so alarmed, *señorita*— the worst is not about to háppen!'

'*Señor!*' Weakness coursed through Laurel's limbs and she groped back into the chair by the desk. 'I—I never expected to—to hear from you,' she stammered. 'I couldn't think who——'

'I felt I had been neglectful too long of my guests,' he broke in smoothly. 'I trust all is well at the *castillo?*'

'Yes, thank you.' Suddenly she felt tongue-tied.

'And my grandmother?'

'She is well, and looking forward to your return.'

'Tell her I will be returning tomorrow, and Tia Costenza is coming home with me.'

'Yes,' she said obediently, getting over her surprise and secretly hoping he was not about to enquire into the activities of his young cousin during his absence. But it seemed that Carlota was not in his thoughts at that moment. Laurel heard her own name, then the line began to crackle and fade and for a moment she thought the call had been cut altogether. Then the interference cleared, and she said anxiously, 'Hello ...?'

'I am still with you.' The mocking note was back in his voice. 'So I am to take it that no one has missed me unduly, *señorita.*'

'Oh, no!' Laurel bit her lip on too undue fervency. 'I'm sure that would be a mistaken assumption. But, *señor* ...'

'Yes, *señorita?*'

'Was there something you wished me to do—perhaps a special message to pass on before your return?'

'No, *señorita.* I have already given José instructions.'

There was another pause, and she said awkwardly, 'I was just wondering, because ...'

'Because why?'

'Well, this call will be costing you a fortune.'

He laughed softly. 'You are concerned about my pocket?'

'Yes, of course.'

'That is a new experience for me. One I find un-expectedly pleasant.' A different inflection had subtly changed his tone, then he added, 'Or perhaps it is that I am enjoying the lilt of a sweet young English voice.'

She felt the warmth of pleasure radiate through her entire being and she glanced around the shadowy room, suddenly glad that only painted eyes were present to witness the flush of rose she knew was tinting her cheeks.

'So you see, *señorita*, I am not entirely unaware that my own people do tend to be a trifle strong-voiced at times.'

On a little surge of mirth she wanted to exclaim that his admission was the understatement of the century, but she could not bear to shatter the delicate warmth of the moment—nor did she know how far to test his humour!

'But I have reduced you to silence!' he broke in before she could frame a suitable response. 'Perhaps it is time for me to heed your wise adjunct and bid you *adiós. Buenos noches, señorita.* Until tomorrow.'

'Until tomorrow,' she whispered, and heard the line close.

She felt superbly happy when she returned to her unfinished coffee and liqueur. The two girls gave her curious glances, but she had no intention of satisfying their curiosity, and the Condesa was too perfect a lady to make even the slightest allusion to the subject of Laurel's phone call. However, Yvonne had no such inhibitions and she followed Laurel into her room when they finally retired upstairs.

'Was that my father?'

'No.'

'Who, then?'

Sighing, Laurel told her, and Yvonne's eyes widened with mischief. 'I guessed! What did he want?'

'To say he was coming home tomorrow.'

'Is that all? Pull the other one! Come on, Laurie, give!'

'There's nothing to give.'

'No?' Yvonne sprawled herself comfortably across Laurel's bed and grinned. 'Have you fallen for him?'

'Of course not.' Laurel turned away, hoping her voice was not giving away the truth. Suddenly a shaft of wisdom made her attack. 'What would you say if I told you he wanted a full account of how you and Carlota have behaved yourselves?'

The grin vanished from Yvonne's face. 'He didn't!' A ghost of the grin reappeared. 'He wouldn't waste long-distance call time on that when he could ask the questions in person tomorrow.'

Laurel repressed a sigh. 'He probably will.'

'So what?' Yvonne looked unabashed. 'We're not worried.'

'So it seems. Tell me,' Laurel frowned, 'how was Carlota so sure that he wouldn't change his plans and land home in time to find you both missing? I mean, it doesn't matter so much about you, but I understood that Carlota's stay here is in the nature of a punishment visit,' she added dryly.

Yvonne's eyes took on a knowing look. 'She knew he would wait for her Aunt Costenza, who lives here, though we haven't met her yet. And Carlota saw her aunt before she left Spain and her aunt said she was going to some special concert on the eighteenth—that's today—so they couldn't leave before tomorrow.'

'I see.' Laurel frowned again, aware of a niggle of puzzlement. 'But I still don't see how she expects to keep any secrets from him. Somebody, one of the servants or someone in the village even, is bound to mention it, even if unintentionally. And I have a feeling he'll be furious.'

Yvonne shrugged. 'Carlota isn't worried, even if he does. She's not afraid of him.'

'Isn't she?'

'Why should she be?' Yvonne exclaimed with a hint of scorn for what she obviously considered naïveté on the part of Laurel. 'Didn't you know? She's an heiress. She's got a fortune coming to her.'

'Yes, I did know.' Laurel bit her lip, aware of something faintly disturbing about this. 'But I don't see what that has to do with it.'

'Don't you?' The knowing expression flitted across Yvonne's face again. She lowered her voice. 'Carlota says he wants to be sure that her fortune stays in the family and she reckons that he'll go along with the family wishes and marry her when she's a year or so older. Otherwise he'd have married already. Do you know how old he is?'

'No.'

'Thirty-four. And he hasn't exactly ignored the feminine sex, according to Carlota. So what else is he waiting for?'

Laurel made no answer. She was discovering that an answer to that careless question was the last thing she wanted to find.

'But Carlota's not sure whether she wants to or not.'

'Isn't she?' Laurel said faintly.

'Well, do you blame her? He'll never leave Destino —he's uncrowned king here—but can you imagine Carlota being cooped up here for the rest of her life?'

'No, I suppose not.' Laurel knew she was being reduced virtually to monosyllables, but she was hearing echoes of the Condesa's words on the very same subject. 'Does—does she love him?' she asked unsteadily.

Yvonne shrugged again. 'I don't think love comes into it. You know what the traditions of these old grandee families are like. They keep the estates together, the women stay home and raise the *chiquillos*, and the men go out and have fun. All the same,' Yvonne giggled, 'she likes making him jealous.'

Does she? Laurel whispered soundlessly to herself as she began mechanically to cream her smooth skin clear of its light film of make-up. All the lovely surge of happiness brought by the Conde's phone call had ebbed away, leaving her chilled and dispirited.

After Yvonne had said goodnight and departed for her own room Laurel climbed into bed and switched off the light. She lay wide awake for a long time, watching the soft billowing movements of the gauzy curtains

as the night breeze wafted in at the open window and
trying to tell herself how foolish she was to feel so
miserable. Because Yvonne's careless confidences should
not have come as any surprise, and, if they were true,
wasn't it natural that a strong-willed, independent girl
like Carlota would be determined not to submit to
tradition as meekly as past generations of the women in
her family probably had? Anyway, Laurel told herself
sadly, it was a logical conclusion that the force of
grandee tradition would eventually surmount even
the forceful Carlota's own secret hopes and desires. If
the Conde had made up his mind to take her as his
bride it was unlikely that anything would stand in his
way. He was that kind of man. And if he made up his
mind to win her love as well as her fortune how would
Carlota ever resist him? What woman could?

CHAPTER NINE

By the next morning Laurel's head was telling her firmly that it was time she kept her mind strictly on her job and the return home at the end of the week. That once back in dear old London, among her friends, occupied with the familiar office routine, Destino and its autocratic grandee would soon recede to the realm of a dream, a dream which would probably haunt her for quite a while, but with the kind of wistfulness she would recognise as belonging strictly in the realm of dreams. She bathed and made ready for the new day with all this in mind, trying to ignore the persistent message of excitement that her heartbeat kept drumming out; *today he was coming back* ...

The girls went riding as usual, and the Condesa announced her intention of resting most of the day in order to husband her frail strength for the excitement of her family returning and the celebration at the *castillo* the next evening.

There was already a great deal of noise and bustle about the place as the servants started the preparations, and José was out in the grounds, supervising the fixing of strings of gaily coloured lanterns in the trees and the torches which would glow in the ancient iron brackets along the walls of the *castillo*. There seemed little place for Laurel, and she decided to make her own preliminary pilgrimage to the shrine that morning. Sofia packed a small picnic lunch for her and she set off up the long winding track into the hills.

It was a beautiful fresh morning. The sea was a brilliant sparkling blue and the sky cloudless, with just enough breeze to temper the heat of the sun, and soon Laurel began to experience a sense of freedom that was unexpectedly pleasant, as though by being alone in the open she gained a respite from emotions fast becoming too disturbing for peace of mind.

She did not hurry, pausing every so often to look back and appreciate the new vista which each turn of the track presented, and she came upon her destination sooner than she had expected. She saw the little chapel first, set back in a natural curve in the hillside and sheltered by a group of pines, and just beyond it was the cave.

It was little more than a deep fissure in the rock, approached by a short flight of narrow, roughly hewn steps, by the side of which ran the channel carrying the thin silvery stream of crystal clear water.

Laurel ascended the steps slowly, aware of a certain stillness in the air and the atmosphere of a hallowed place. It was very simple and very wonderful; white candles set in metal sconces on a ledge at the back of the cave which formed a natural altar, and a small painted statue of the Virgin above the cleft in the rock from where the water spilled. Only the soft musical trickle of the spring broke the silence, and Laurel stood for a little while, filled with that strange sense of peace humility can bring, before she came back out of the dimness to the brilliance of the day and a view that almost took away her breath.

The island lay like a green map below, studded with the farms and the houses of the little port by the edge of the blue crystal ocean. To one side she could see the deep shadowy verdance of the citrus groves, and hear the calls of a boy down in the valley as he shepherded his flock to their pasture. Further away a horse plodded along a track, its cart laden with baskets of produce, heading for the market place, and Laurel was able to pick out the white villa where she had stayed when they first arrived on the island. How far away in time it seemed now. She sighed and turned her head, shading her eyes against the sun, and saw to her left the great shape of the *castillo* dominating the headland, and indeed the island. How many youthful brides had it received within its walls, held their happiness or their fate down the centuries? What would it feel like to walk into its gracious gardens and its cool grandeur and call it home?

Laurel sighed again and picked up her basket. She retraced her steps a little way down the hill until she came to a suitable spot in which to partake of her lunch. Sofia had packed the basket generously. There were little chicken-filled rolls wrapped in cool lettuce, snack biscuits with cheese and olives and a couple of hard-boiled eggs, some fruit and half a bottle of light wine. Enough for two at least, Laurel thought as she threw crumbs from the roll she couldn't eat to the hopefully hovering birds. When she had finished she lay back, feeling the sun pleasurably warm on her face, and allowed her thoughts to wander ... But the sight of her own folder of notes about the island brought an abruptly sobering effect.

If tourism should come to the island how would it affect the peace and simplicity she was enjoying at this very moment? Her imagination threw up a picture of the little chapel and the shrine, made tawdry by stalls hung about with garish souvenirs and gimmicky tourist wares. Perhaps even the precious water would become a ware, for human nature, no matter how well-meaning, was very frail ...

Laurel sat up, her eyes troubled. If only visitors could come as she had, accepting the island as it was, and leaving it unchanged. But it wasn't as simple as that ... She began to pack the picnic things back into the basket and folded the green-checked cloth. Then a movement caught her eye and she forgot her troublesome thoughts. The steamer was coming in.

It was still quite a long way out, and she sat there motionless, her heartbeat quickening, watching the vessel cleave its way across the blue expanse, gradually becoming more distinguishable as it neared the harbour. Very soon it would dock, and Laurel was possessed of an urge to grab up her things and race down the track as fast as her feet would carry her, back into the spell of those walls below and the owner who made the real magic of Destino.

Laurel fought down the traitorous urge; let the Conde come home and greet his family without strangers to intrude. She forced herself to remain there at her vantage point until the steamer lay achored by the quay and time enough had passed for the Conde to disembark. Doubtless José would be meeting him, the Condesa would be waiting for her grandson and Tia Costenza, and a meal would be ready.

Laurel took her time, and made her way back to the *castillo* by a more roundabout way. She was quite tired and hot by the time she arrived, and all seemed quiet when she walked into the welcome coolness of the main hall. She put her folder and personal things on a settle and went through to the kitchen to return the picnic basket. A shower would be welcome now, and a change into something cool and fresh . . .

She heard the raised voices the moment she re-entered the hall. They came in a torrent of Spanish from the doorway of the *sala*, and Laurel stiffened; this was not excitable Spanish, this was very angry Spanish. She drew back a step, hesitating to pass the open door-way, then she saw Yvonne just within the room, stand-ing there with a half-frightened expression on her face. The next moment Carlota emerged, her features con-torted with fury. She stopped short as she saw Laurel in the hall, then she ran forward.

'It was you!' she accused. 'You told him! Now I know why you looked so pleased with yourself last night. How dare you interfere in affairs which do not concern you?' she stormed. 'Why do you make trouble for me? You have——'

'Carlota! Be silent this instant!'

The Conde stood in the doorway behind her, his face a mask of tightly controlled anger. 'You will apolo-gise. Now!' he said icily.

'No!' Carlota whirled to face him. 'Do you think I am a child? To be ordered about and chastised like any stupid *niña*? I——'

'*Carlota!*' he seized her arm and caught the other furious hand that came up like a flail towards his face.

'If you behave like a child you will be treated like one. How dare you attack a guest in this way and make such unfounded accusations? You——'

'Unfounded!' she spat. 'You brought her here to spy on me, didn't you? And you talk of——'

'You are wrong!' The dark fury in his eyes surpassed even the stormy rage in Carlota's incensed face. 'Miss Daneway was *not* the source of my information regarding your foolish and disobedient escapade. Now apologise—instantly!'

'But who ...' A sullen astonishment stilled the Spanish girl's struggles to free herself from his merciless grip. 'No one else has been with us—since your return. No one else has talked with us. So how——?'

'It seems my word does not convince you,' he said angrily. 'You appear to forget that the world is made small by transport and communications in this modern age. This morning I met, purely by accident, Senhor and Senhora Pereira. They were on their way to visit Senhora Pereira's sister in Madrid before flying to Lisbon for a holiday. It is perhaps unfortunate for you, Carlota, that they happened to see you during your jaunt to Funchal. And I begin to feel that their genuine regret in not being allowed to entertain you and your young friend is sadly misplaced. Now,' he added grimly, 'I am waiting.'

Carlota's red mouth tightened and she shot a glance of sheer malevolence towards Laurel before she glared defiantly at the Conde's implacable face. 'You will have to wait, then, Rodrigo,' she cried. 'You have humiliated *me*! But that does not matter! Oh, no! *I* am humiliated, but *I* must make the apologies. Well, I will not. Never! I did not want to come here—but what do I find when I do? A spy! A spy to watch over all my actions. And you expect me to——'

'Carlota! Rodrigo!'

The firm, clear voice brought abrupt silence. The Condesa stood in the hall, displeasure chilling her fine-boned old face. Beside her hovered a plump, middle-aged woman with grey threading her dark hair. She looked fretful and distressed as well as disapproving. The Condesa moved forward stiffly, still as straight as a ramrod despite her need of the silver-topped ebony cane. She surveyed her grandchildren coldly.

'Must you brawl like *campesinos*?'

The Conde's face closed. He drew himself to his full height and inclined his head to his grandmother. '*Perdone usted*, Abuela,' he said formally.

The Condesa nodded. 'In future,' she said tartly, 'confine family arguments to the family circle, and spare our unfortunate guests such unwonted embarrassment. Carlota, I wish to speak to you. Go to my sitting room and await me there.'

To Laurel's surprise, the Spanish girl turned meekly at that authoritative command and went silently across the hall towards the door to the Condesa's suite. The old lady gave her grandson a brief nod that conveyed something very like warning before she turned slowly, only then accepting the arm of Tia Costenza.

Yvonne was still standing in the background, something suspiciously like a giggle struggling round her mouth. Laurel took a warning step towards her, and found her way barred.

The Conde looked down at her, the remoteness of a stranger in his eyes. 'There is something I wish to say to you, *señorita*. You will permit me to detain you for a few moments?'

The words were spoken with impeccable courtesy but the chill command behind them was unmistakable. Suddenly Laurel felt as though something precious had withered and died. She swallowed painfully, determined that dignity should triumph over the instant desire to argue, and followed his indicative gesture towards the open door of his study. Was this what she had looked forward to, dreamed of, last night?

When he had closed the door she said stiffly: 'Well, *señor*?'

'Why did you disobey my instructions?' he demanded without preamble.

'Disobey?' Her lips stayed parted with astonishment.

She had known since the first glimpse of his expression that she was included in his displeasure, and she was fully prepared for an inquisition regarding the two girls' behaviour. But she was not prepared for the arrant censure, accusation even, that was patent now in every line of his attitude.

His dark eyes blazed with scarcely repressed anger. 'Come now, Miss Daneway. You are surely not so naïve as to pretend you do not grasp my meaning. How dare you permit my cousin and your young charge to flout my wishes so blatantly?'

'How dare I——? But I didn't——' Laurel bit her lip, unwilling to implicate the girls further even at the expense of her own defence. 'I——'

'You did not give your permission?' he said sharply.

'I certainly did not give them permission to flout your wishes deliberately,' she said flatly.

'Then why did you allow them to leave the island the moment I was absent?'

Laurel felt her temper sliding. 'Do you think it's as simple as that?' she cried. 'Do you really believe that two sixteen-year-old girls will accept that kind of rigid dictatorship in this day and age? Just because you are technically head of the family and one day you expect to——'

She bit back her unwary tongue, and he said quickly: 'One day I expect what, señorita?'

'You expect to rule Carlota's life, regardless of her own desires, because it has always been the tradition. How do you imagine she feels? Do you ever try to see her point of view?' Laurel asked fiercely. 'Why don't you try reasoning with her for a change instead of treating her like a child?'

'A wilful girl of that age is incapable of reasoning—as I believed you had already discovered. However,' his mouth set in a grim line, 'I am at risk of forgetting you are a guest under my roof and dealing with you as you deserve. We will say no more of the matter.'

Laurel gasped. It was all of five years since a particularly sarcastic headmaster had made her feel as small and as furious as she felt at this moment. Deliberately she placed herself between the Conde and the door he was about to open for her own suitably chastened exit. 'But *I* haven't finished!' she exclaimed hotly. 'I think the greatest mistake was my ever allowing myself to become a guest under your roof. I should have trusted my first impression and stayed as far from Castillo Valderosa as possible!'

'And what was that first impression?' he said in dangerously quiet tones.

'That you were cold, hard and arrogant, and uncaring of anyone's feelings who failed to conform to your hidebound grandee tradition!' she flared. 'All I can say is that I'm sorry for Carlota.'

His eyes burned with the glints of tempered steel. 'That is all you have to say, *señorita*?'

Laurel felt a tremor of sick fear. There was whiteness in the creases at the corners of his mouth and a dangerous tautness in the set of his jaw. Suddenly she perceived the dark violence he was holding under tightly leashed control. She stared back resolutely. 'Yes—I don't think there is anything left to say, *señor*.'

'Except for one thing,' he gritted. 'Perhaps I too was mistaken in a certain impression. I too made an error of judgment.'

'In what way?'

'I put a trust where it appears to have been sadly misplaced, *señorita*.'

Afterwards, Laurel never knew how she managed to walk out of that room and the Conde's chill, implacable presence with her head held high, nor how she managed to get through the rest of that day.

There were several guests for dinner that evening, but despite the presence of Don Amadeo, the island's priest, Señor Alvarez, the schoolmaster, and his wife, and the much loved 'Herr Doktor', the German surgeon who had retired to Destino and who gave unstintingly of his time and skill whenever it was needed, there was an air of constraint that even the superb food and wine and the animated discussion of the *romeria* could not dispel for Laurel.

She was painfully aware of the tall, aristocratic man at the head of the table. The play of lamplight on the chiselled planes of his features increased his enigmatic air and made her heart ache merely to look at him. Occasionally his glance would come to rest on her, dark and unfathomable, then glinting with small flame points like rapier thrusts of cruelty when the betraying colour surged up into her cheeks and she wrenched her own glance away. In those moments she told herself fiercely that she hated him, even as she recognised the hopelessness of the attempt at self-delusion.

She was thankful when the long evening drew at last to its close. The guests prepared to depart, the Condesa bade them all goodnight, and Laurel escaped to the solitude of her room. Her head had begun to ache with the effect of rich food and a little too much wine drunk from sheer unhappiness, and there was a tight, smarting sensation in her eyes that resisted all attempts to blink it away.

She crept miserably into bed, to close her eyes and try to make her mind a blank, except for one more pitiful little delusion: that tomorrow, amidst all the excitement and the crowds, she would surely be able to avoid that disturbing presence and those censorious eyes ...

But she could only lie there and dream hopelessly of those eyes warm and challenging and compelling, and a mouth whose warm magic could make havoc of all resistance ...

*   *   *

The excitement began at dawn.

After early Mass the children spilled out over the island to gather fragrant blossoms with which to decorate the church and the special litter on which the

Virgin would be carried in the triumphal procession to the Shrine later in the day. At eleven the church bells began their summons, and up at the *castillo* the Conde's party prepared to set off for the special service which would precede the pilgrimage.

Laurel looked cool and beautiful in her white dress as she waited in the courtyard. Unhappiness had etched troubled little shadows under her eyes and lent her an air of remoteness that was strangely appealing. But she was unaware of her appearance; she was painfully conscious of the invisible wall that had risen between herself and the Conde. This morning she wished with all her heart she had the means of demolishing the barrier, but each time she stole a glance at his dark, impassive features she despaired of the impossibility of achieving that hopeless aim. The omens for the day were not good so far!

Her advent at breakfast had silenced what sounded like a full-scale family argument. She had drawn back, instantly aware of the Conde's sharp glance towards her and the icy formality in the inclination of his head towards her as he bade her good morning. She had hesitated still, and the Condesa had called with a hint of impatience, 'Come, child—you should know by now that we sound much worse than we are!'

'I'm sorry,' she stammered, 'I didn't mean to be late.'

'No, *señorita*, it is we who are early,' the Conde said.

His smooth, urbane tone made the words a meaningless politeness and Laurel felt worse than ever as she took her place at the table. The silence now seemed unnatural, centred round herself, then Carlota smiled maliciously.

'I'm sure Miss Daneway is still under the impression that we are about to come to blows when we are merely discussing the weather.'

The spiteful little dig was unfair and unwarranted, and Tia Costenza's instant rebuke did little to dispel the sting of it, nor did the Conde's brusque, 'But we were not discussing the weather.'

The Condesa looked at her grandson and her black

eyes snapped with temper. 'I forbid another word on the matter! It is decided. I wish to attend church this morning and I have every intention of doing so. My——'

'But, Madre, the crowds and the excitement!' Tia Costenza waved her hands. 'You know it will be too much for you! Last year you——'

'This is this year!' The Condesa turned a quelling glance on her daughter. 'Must you make me feeble in the head as well as body? My accursed infirmity and the cosseting of my family have prevented me from joining the pilgrimage these past five years, but it is not going to imprison me today like the enfeebled old crone you would make me. Now, Rodrigo,' her chin jutted up, 'are you going to escort me in the car? Or must I instruct José to resurrect the old carriage?'

The Conde bowed his head. 'That will not be necessary, Abuelita. I am at your command.'

'Thank you.' The Condesa's smile was acid with triumph. Now that she had gained her own way the tension began to ease out of the atmosphere and a typical family discussion began as to whether the Conde should first take his grandmother and aunt to the church and then return for the girls or the other way round. Laurel instantly said she would walk, echoed by Yvonne and followed by vehement protests from the two older ladies, and the Conde held up his hand with a weary gesture for silence.

'You will not walk, señorita,' he ordained. 'You will drive, as befitting a guest with the castillo party.'

The expression on his face did not invite argument, and Laurel said quietly, 'As you think best, señor.' But now, watching him help the indomitable old lady to settle herself comfortably in the car, Laurel felt a renewed stiffening of her own spirit. Was she going to let him see the power he held to spoil her happiness? Perhaps even betray feelings she would die rather than ever allow him to perceive? If he chose to be so utterly chill and disapproving then she would be equally remote. For his attitude was completely unfair, she told

herself. After all, he had practically forced her to become his guest, and had thrust on her, virtually a
stranger in his household, a responsibility almost impossible to carry. Then he had taken her to task when
she failed through no fault of her own. No, she decided,
she would not let him spoil her day, nor give him the
satisfaction of knowing how deeply he had hurt her;
she would put on the greatest pretence of her life . . .

The nature of the day made it easier than she had
expected. There was so much colour and movement
and noise, and a wild fervency of joy and ardour that
caught at the heart with a strange poignancy. No one
was at work that day, and the town wore a clean-
scrubbed, festive air. No washing strung across balconies
now, only bright flowers in the window boxes and
massed in pots on every available ledge, and the chir-
ruping of pet birds fluffing their colourful plumage in
the ornamental cages hung outside some of the houses.
Everybody wore Sunday best; the men in sober dark
suits, little girls excited and pretty in white dresses
and small boys constrained and polished for once in
more formal wear, and the women in flower-hued
summery dresses with light scarves covering their heads.
Only the older women stayed faithful to their normal
black garb, with little lace mantillas hiding their hair
as they joined the crowd converging on the square.

The church was packed, hot and scented with in-
cense and the starry clusters of many candles, strung
like necklaces about the church and shining on the
figure of the Virgin in her special festal robes of blue
and silver and rose.

There were not enough seats for everyone and there
was much good-humoured to-ing and fro-ing in
search of additional chairs. Some of the children had
to sit on cushions at the front, and nobody minded the
considerable amount of scuffling and adjusting of
cushions that went on during the service.

When it was over the great moment came for which
all had eagerly awaited, when the statue of the Virgin
was carried reverently out of the church, serene upon

her specially decorated litter. It was white and gold, with four tall slender poles supporting a white silk canopy encrusted with gold and silver beadwork, and the children scrambled and jostled to place their tender little offerings of posies around the hem of her robes while the town band formed at the head of the procession and the men who were to be the first four bearers took their places at the four corners of the litter.

At last they moved off, amid an incredible babble of voices and dancing children, across the square and through the little town, and on to the winding track that led up to the shrine in the hills. Every so often the procession halted to enable fresh bearers to take up the litter, and then they would move on again. Carlota and Yvonne had been quickly lost in the crowd and on several occasions Laurel found herself completely separated from her companions. But always she was able to pick out the tall figure of the Conde, his dark head unmistakable and his glance sometimes sweeping around in search of his party. Beyond this, he made no attempt to keep the *castillo* party near him, and Laurel tried not to feel hurt that he remained so formal. She forced herself to smile brilliantly and laugh with the island folk around her each time she sensed his gaze turn in her direction.

When the pilgrimage reached the shrine and the *ermita*, which was much too small to accommodate the crowd, the priest conducted a brief, more informal service of thanksgiving and blessing which somehow became much more moving in its simplicity beneath blue skies than had the principal service in the church.

And then it was over. After the return to the town and the restoring of the Virgin to her niche in the church the procession broke up and dispersed, to prepare joyfully for the evening's revels.

Back at the *castillo* there was a belated light meal and the last-minute preparations for the invasion, as Yvonne termed it. Everyone was pressed into service, helping to carry out the buffet tables and the endless trays of food and dishes and all the necessities for the largest picnic Laurel had ever known. When at last everything was in readiness there was just time for a quick refreshing shower and change into festive finery. Laurel vaguely noticed that someone had brought up her forgotten belongings, left down in the hall the previous afternoon just before the heartbreak encounter which had driven all thought of them out of her head. She bundled them into her wardrobe and took down the white lace evening top and long, dark red skirt she was going to wear. It was an outfit she had worn several times, and one in which she had always been happy; her heart dared to quicken its beat hopefully; perhaps it would work its magic again ...

Already the islanders were streaming up the track to the *castillo*. Old and young, girls like bright butterflies in their finery, some of the men in skin-fitting velvet suits with vivid flaunting ruffles cascading down their shirt-fronts. A glorious smell of roasting lamb, suckling pig and spit-roasted chicken hung in the air. The buffet tables groaned under the weight of mouthwatering arrays of savouries, pastries, every kind of sweetmeat nibbles one could think of, and of course wines. Lamps glowed romantically among the trees, the night was warm and perfect, and the noise was incredible.

Moonrise found Laurel alone and bemused by it all, standing near the end of one of the buffet tables. Yvonne had just left her, to go in search of someone to dance with, after announcing that she couldn't eat another thing and if she didn't dance it all down she'd burst. Laurel felt similar sentiments; she didn't think she would want to eat anything else for a month.

'Try this, *señorita*.'

She gave a start of shock as the tall shadow fell across her path and the voice she had not expected at that moment issued its soft, beguiling invitation. Her mouth forgot to form its bright, uncaring smile as she looked up at the Conde's suave, enigmatic features. 'What are they?' she asked rather unsteadily over the dish of confectionery he proffered.

'*Mazapán* from Toledo—it is a speciality of the almond. A confection the English are also partial to, I believe.'

'Thank you.' She tried not to look at the glint of white teeth between those devastating chiselled lips as she bit into the rich sweetmeat. 'It is very good,' she acknowledged in a stiff little voice.

'You are enjoying yourself?'

Just as though nothing had happened! 'Very much.' She regained her self-possession and flashed him a polite smile. 'The gardens look very beautiful.'

He inclined his head formally, but before he could respond José materialised at his elbow, looking anxious. The Conde was drawn away to attend to some unforeseen hitch, and Laurel took a deep breath to settle her disturbed heartbeats. She wandered on through the vociferous crowd, past the clusters of ·islanders who grouped round small tables dotted round the perimeter of the garden or sat picnic fashion under the trees enjoying their alfresco meal. Suddenly a voice exclaimed, 'Laurel, you look lost, *niña mía!* Come and sit down and tell me about the pilgrimage.'

The Condesa was holding court in an arbour which commanded an unbroken view of the section of the terrace set apart for the performance which would begin very soon. Already the musicians were gathering at one side, and banks of flowers had been massed on the shallow steps. Coloured lanterns glowed like the loops of a necklace overhead, and above it all the moon was rising to begin her silvery glide across the midnight blue heavens.

It was a romantic scene, dominated by the great stone mass of the *castillo* making a fantastic backdrop to the scene, and Laurel sighed without realising it as she obeyed the Condesa's behest. Misreading the sigh, the Condesa made a 'Tchk-tchk' exclamation of concern. 'You sound weary, my child. Is no one looking after you? Ramon!' She snapped her fingers and a young manservant appeared solicitously. 'Bring some more wine and a glass for the *señorita*.'

Laurel discovered she was thankful to sink into the chair; she had not realised how exhausting the day had been. She accepted the wine gratefully and relaxed back, glad of the shadows within the arbour and a strange sense of immunity lent by the Condesa's presence. She answered the Condesa's questions, and presently the garden lamps dimmed and floodlights sprang to life above the impromptu stage on the terrace. A moment later six dancers ran into the floodlit circle. The guitars throbbed a rich plangency of melody, castanets beat out their intricate rhythm, the brilliant hues of the dancers' frilled skirts whirled a kaleidoscope of colour, and the performance began. They danced to a long medley of favourite old Spanish pieces, and Laurel marvelled at their seemingly inexhaustible energy. Singers followed, and then a strikingly handsome male dancer made his entrance, to dance a dramatic bolero to the famous music of Ravel. The applause was rapturous when he finished, sweat making his face glisten like polished teak as he stood whipcord-slim in black receiving his ovation.

'I didn't know your island possessed such talent—he's wonderful!' Laurel exclaimed to the Condesa as she clapped enthusiastically.

'Alas, the island does not.'

The voice came from behind, and it was not the Condesa's. Laurel quivered as hands rested on the back of her chair, brushing her shoulders on the way. How long had he stood there?

'These dancers come from Madrid—they arrived only this morning and will return tomorrow,' the Conde said above her head.

'Oh, I didn't know.' Laurel's reply was stiff. She felt foolish and ignorant. How could she not have realised that such a superb performance could come only from a highly professional troupe?

The singers had returned to the stage, and Laurel sat stiffly upright, illogical resentment making her determined to avoid any risk of the slightest bodily contact with the man standing behind her chair. She remained thus through the last two items, all pleasure gone, and as soon as the performance ended she murmured a polite excuse to the Condesa and escaped. Her pretext was valid enough, she told herself when she reached her room; she felt overheated, sticky and untidy, and in need of a refreshing wash. That done, she applied a light make-up and slowly made her way back to the festivities.

The more formal part of the evening had ended now and taped music was being played through invisible amplifiers concealed about the grounds. Dancing had begun for those who wished it and most of the crowd seemed to be taking part, watched by the older and less energetic folk now relaxing and exchanging their anecdotes of the day. Laurel found a secluded place in a corner at the far end of the terrace and leaned on the balustrade watching the swirl of movement below. There was no sign of Yvonne, but she caught a glimpse of Carlota, who was dancing with the young male virtuoso who had given such a memorable performance earlier on. He appeared as equally interested in Carlota as she seemed to be in him, and watching their enrapt faces in those few moments before they were lost to sight brought an unexpected pang to Laurel's heart. Suddenly she felt unutterably lonely.

She sighed, wondering if she was the only one to feel so weary and lost on this festive night, the high spot of Destino's year. What a fool she was, to let her heart rule her head this way! Drooping here like a lovelorn adolescent. Why couldn't she . . .

'So this is where you hide yourself, *señorita*!'

A gasp escaped her and she spun round. The Conde stood there, immaculate in his dark velvet jacket, moonlight casting metallic silver lights amid the deep planes and shadows of his features.

'I—I'm not hiding, *señor*,' she denied. 'Why—why should I?'

'Why indeed! You will permit me the honour of dancing with you, *señorita*?'

'I—I——' Laurel bit her lip. Half of her mind said

run while she could; the other half yearned to rush into his arms. But his hand had closed round her wrist, and like someone not quite in possession of all senses she felt herself drawn along the terrace and down the shallow steps to be taken in his arms and merged among the other dancers.

'Relax,' he murmured silkily, 'and do not try to convince me you are unable to dance. It is very easy, in the old-fashioned way, like they dance in the old movies. How do you call it?—cheek-to-cheek?'

Laurel could not think of anything more desirable —or dangerous—at that moment. 'I—I don't think they dance that way now,' she said rather wildly.

'And *I* do not think there is any set rule about it,' he said in the same smooth tones. His arm seemed to tighten more about her waist. 'Now try to look as though you do not hate me, *señorita*.'

'I—I wasn't aware that I looked like—that way,' she said on a note of hysteria.

'No? Your eyes have held a passable imitation of it today, *señorita*.' He paused, his own eyes unfathomable. 'I should prefer to hear your own contradiction of that impression.'

'Of course I don't hate you,' she said in a choked whisper.

'I am thankful to hear it. Perhaps you will tell me now why you have been avoiding me all day.'

'But I haven't.'

'No?' He swayed her expertly, his steps faultless, and despite her determination to remain cool and unyielding at all cost Laurel felt her traitor body melting to the lean hard pressure of masculine contours moulding her own.

And the music wasn't exactly helping her resolution. Well-loved romantic Latin themes; *South of the Border* ... *Andalucia* ... and the haunting, sensuous strains of *Spanish Eyes* in a languorous tempo that could take dancing over the border into lovemaking before the unwary dancer realised what was happening ...

'Then I must conclude that perhaps you were sulking,' he said softly against her temple.

Laurel's heart was thudding so hard she was positive he could both hear and feel it. 'I think you were mistaken, *señor*.' She turned her head from that disturbing contact, to stare stubbornly across his shoulder. 'There has not been much opportunity today to talk to you.'

'That is not the answer I seek.'

She thought she detected amusement in his tone, and a tremor ran through her. Suddenly she could not endure any more of this torment. How dared he start to flirt and amuse himself at her expense as though his anger of last night had never happened? She missed a beat, stumbled, and broke free of his hold. 'Very well,' she cried, 'I *will* give you your answer! Yes, I was angry all day. Did you expect anything else after the way you spoke to me last night? As though I were one of your *peóns* who had committed some misdemeanour that displeased Your Highness! And now you seem to expect me to fall into your arms and behave like a deferential guest as if nothing had happened. Well, I won't! Find someone else to dance with, *señor*!'

Shaken by her own outburst, she turned blindly away from the dancers and stumbled into the dimness of a path beneath the trees. Almost immediately there was the embarrassment of a pair of lovers and she turned away, seeking her bearings, the identity of the couple not registering until a muttered, extremely unladylike profanity reached her ears and she remembered the glimpse of crimson voile and luminous white within the black shadows. Yvonne! And she was with——!

Laurel whirled round, just in time to see Yvonne's guilty disengagement from Renaldo's arms. For a moment she forgot everything but anger. Much of her present unhappy predicament stemmed from Yvonne's indiscretion with the young philanderer of the guest house, and now Yvonne was ... But as Laurel voiced a sharp cry she felt her shoulders seized from behind and she was pulled round to face the Conde. She had a blurred impression of Renaldo and Yvonne removing themselves rapidly from the scene before her captor's impatient features blotted out everything else.

'*Dios mio!* Let them go!' he exclaimed, almost shaking her to silence her agitated protests. 'I am beginning to weary of troublesome young *niñas* and their even more troublesome *amantes*. And so should you, *señorita*. Why do you always run from me before anything can be resolved?'

'Is there anything worth resolving?' she asked bitterly.

Suddenly she was close to tears, and when he snapped: 'What answer is that?' she turned her head away and made a despairing attempt to master her emotions. 'It means that I *am* weary, *señor*. But not quite in the way you are.'

'And what is that supposed to convey?'

'That I'm tired of being forced to switch on and off,' she cried. 'One moment to the formality of distant acquaintances and the next to your anger and accusations. And then—and then——'

'And then?' he prompted, his mouth thinning.

Her chin lifted defiantly and she stared directly at him. 'Being expected to behave as though none of it happened when you feel like playing Don Juan!'

'Don Juan!'

His teeth glinted like white fire through the violent exclamation and his fingers bit into her shoulders with the strength of forged steel. Laurel braced herself for the storm which must surely be the reaction to her rash outburst, and the moment of appalling silence seemed to stretch to eternity. Then unbelievably the tension of coiled steel relaxed on her soft flesh and she felt the soft, sibilant whisper of his breath escape warm against her cheek.

'*Por Dios!* Is that how you see me?'

He was shaking his head, and Laurel felt the old traitorous weakness pervading her limbs. It was all she could do to remain in control of her balance and not sag limply against him. She said unevenly, 'I—I think I have had provocation, *señor*.'

'And I have not, of course.' The sardonic note in his

voice made her drop her gaze. She looked down stubbornly, wishing she had the strength to break away and
end this cat-and-mouse game which she hadn't a hope
of winning. Then his hand moved swiftly to her throat
and one lean finger curved under her chin, forcing it
up till she could not evade his gaze. 'No, *señorita*, I
fear that not even my enemies would make such an
accusation—unless wanting to kiss you and hold you
in my arms until those shadows of hurt cease to darken
your eyes qualifies me for the role of our legendary
rake.'

Laurel trembled and sought wildly for words that
would not come. He was imperceptibly drawing her
closer and she knew she was powerless to resist. In a
moment she would be reaching up with her own
arms ... 'I—I am not hurt, *señor*,' she said in a
strangled little voice. 'I—I just want to—to——'

'Yes ...?' His finger-tips had found the secret curve
under her hairline at the nape of her neck and his
thumb played gently with the lobe of her ear. 'There is
something you wish, Señorita Laurel?'

'I—I must find where Yvonne's got to,' she said
wildly, 'in case——'

'In case the worst has happened! Stay your fear—
by now Renaldo will be as far as possible from your
charge, doubtless wooing some other foolish little
señorita.'

'But how can you tell?'

'Because he will not forget my displeasure in a hurry.'
A vein of steel hardened the masterful voice. 'I can
assure you that he will not risk incurring my wrath for
a long time to come.'

The shadows failed to conceal the grim expression
that flitted across his features and Laurel shivered as
she remembered that encounter with Renaldo. She
whispered, 'I hope not.'

'A memory troubles you?'

'Only for a moment.'

'Forget it,' he urged, soft yet insistent. 'This is the

one night of our year when there must be no unhappy memories. Laurie, look at me.'

His voice was as warm and caressing as velvet, and a heady excitement coursed through her like wine in her veins. She could no more resist the whispered diminutive of her name on his lips than she could break free of the spell in which he was weaving her captive.

'I want to see that look of unhappiness that you have worn all day banished. I want to ...'

The rest of his desire was transmuted in the descent of his mouth on hers, and there was nothing except the flare of the most exquisite ecstasy she had ever experienced. Her hands found their own way to cradle his dark head while his arms gathered her ever tighter and his hard body seared her from breast to hip, as though it would fuse with her in the heat of desire. He swayed her, trailing the fire of his mouth down the quivering whiteness of her throat, then returning to her mouth until she was drowning in time and space and he was taking her with him into passion's eternity.

When he raised his head she was aware only of being bereft. The voice that spoke from the shadows came from another world and she scarcely heard it and the note of shock betrayed by its owner. In a daze she heard Rodrigo respond and then urge her forward.

'It is time for champagne and our special display ... Come, Laurie *querida* ...'

Querida ... darling! Laurel walked by his side, her toes scarcely touching the ground, and oblivious to the angry darting glances of Carlota, who had come in search of the Conde to bid him return to the *castillo*, where the Condesa and the principal guests awaited his presence.

Champagne magnums nestled in snowy ice within softly gleaming silver buckets, and crystal glasses stood waiting in sparkling clusters on white-clothed tables on the terrace. The first popping cork seemed as though it were a signal and a second later a brilliant star shot heavenwards to burst and drench down over the gardens in a shower of golden rain: a display of fireworks had begun.

Laurel watched entranced as roman candles flared and catherine wheels spun dizzily, and dazzling rockets whizzed up into the black velvet sky, paling the moon and taking her own heart in a gasp of joyous flight. The Conde stood at her side, one arm around her slender waist, and the pressure of his hand sent shivers like electric sparks throbbing through her body. She had never dreamed such happiness could exist . . .

When at last it was over she sighed, wishing that it could have gone on for ever. She sensed rather than saw the Condesa move away and the guests drift down into the garden to rejoin the dancing which was to recommence. The lamps glowed again like fireflies amid the trees and laughter echoed about the *castillo* walls. Children ran among the couples and shrieked with excitement; it was long after midnight, but no one cared.

'Come, we will dance . . .' The Conde waited, and to Laurel there was the promise of heaven in his dark, intent eyes.

She laughed, and turned to put down her crystal glass, and found Carlota standing there, a strangely frightening expression on her vivid oval face. Laurel felt a shiver down her spine, as though someone had walked across her future grave, but Carlota flung her a brilliant smile.

'You will have found all this most interesting, Laurel, have you not? A very special attraction for your spring package deal. Tell me, do you write the material for the brochure?'

'*What?*' Laurel's mouth parted. She could only stare at the Spanish girl while the beginning of horror chilled her heart. 'What do you mean, Carlota?'

'Oh, come, you know very well what I mean! Why do you pretend? It is no secret, is it?'

Carlota turned wide, apparently innocent eyes from Laurel to the Conde, then back to Laurel. She gave a little shake of her head, as though puzzled. 'Why do you draw maps of our island and make many notes about different things concerning us? It is true, is it not, that Yvonne's father is a London travel arranger and you work as his secretary?'

Laurel felt herself sway. From a long way away she heard the Conde give a sharp exclamation, and then Carlota cried: 'But of course it is true, Rodrigo. You mean you did not *know*! That they wish to come here, no doubt to build their holiday camps and their bingoes, and ice cream parlours. They will come in their thousands and tramp all over Destino. But why don't you ask her? She can't deny it! It is her job.'

'*Is this true?*'

Laurel recoiled from the outraged man who stared down into her white face as though he could scarcely believe the disclosures echoing around him. Yvonne's name rushed into Laurel's mind—oh, surely she hadn't forgotten her own frantic pleas for secrecy and told Carlota? Then sick comprehension came with the memory of the folder of notes left in the hall the previous afternoon and forgotten in the events which followed. She said desperately: 'No—let me explain —it isn't quite like that. I never intended——'

'Tell me the truth!' he stormed. 'Do you work for this man? This——'

'His name is Gordon Searle,' Carlota interrupted triumphantly, 'and his business is called Planet Panorama. It is on his notepaper which Miss Daneway so carelessly left lying around for all to see. That is why I am surprised you know nothing of this, Rodrigo,' the Spanish girl added with wide-eyed innocence.

'Do you?' he demanded, as though Carlota had not spoken.

'Yes, but ...' Laurel swallowed hard, trying to subdue the sick misery threatening to choke her. 'I——'

'That is all I need to hear.' His eyes burned with fury and his jawline set like carved teak. 'You have deceived me and abused my hospitality. You——'

'Please ...' Laurel put a desperate hand on his arm, 'please listen, *señor*. I——'

'I do not wish to listen.' He shook her hand away as though it were something distasteful and repugnant. 'I do not wish to hear any more lies from your lips.' He stood very stiffly erect and his mouth thinned to a cruel line. Only the whiteness at his nostrils and the corners of his mouth betrayed the anger he was mastering. 'You will no doubt be wishing to return to England very soon, *señorita*. I am afraid my answer must be as it was to a previous, similar enquiry. I will never permit package tourism or any tourist development on Destino. *Buenas noches, señorita*.'

With the stiff acknowledgement he turned and strode into the *castillo*.

Suddenly Laurel was alone in the shadows. The music, the colour, the noise and the gaiety of fiesta was all around her, unreal, disjointed, the fragments of a world that had shattered like a delicate, precious shell.

Her shell . . . her world . . .

CHAPTER TEN

THAT last day at Castillo Valderosa was the most miserable in Laurel's whole existence, and one that seemed determined to etch itself on her memory for ever. Even when it was all over and she had been back in the old familiar routine for nearly three weeks nothing would banish the memories and the sick leaden feeling stayed heavy round her heart.

If only there had been a way to put things right. All through those last dragging hours she had alternated between dread of coming face to face with the Conde and an agony of longing to see him, to hear his voice again, while she wished with all her heart that somehow, magically, it had never happened.

But it *had* happened, and she had left Destino without seeing him again. He had spent that last day touring the estate and had taken Carlota with him. Oh, he had left a message, saying that the English guests were not to hesitate to avail themselves of the *castillo* telephone should they wish to place a call to London to advise their families of their pending arrival, and should they require anything they were to request it of José, who would drive them down to the quay and assist them with their luggage.

Only the Condesa had wished them '*Feliz viaje*' when Laurel went somewhat timorously to say goodbye and thank her for her kindness. The Condesa had looked sad, and the expression of disappointment in her old eyes had almost reduced Laurel to tears. The only comfort had come from Yvonne, who had tried hard to cheer Laurel during the flight home. Once again the younger girl had surprised her with a warmth of affectionate sympathy. After the disastrous finale to the *romería* Laurel had fully expected blunt censure from Yvonne regarding her carelessness in leaving the damning folder where it could fall into Carlota's hands. But Yvonne had flung impulsive young arms about her, begging her not to be upset and swearing furiously about a certain bitch with black hair who couldn't keep her talons out of other people's personal belongings. She had gone on passionately in this strain until Carlota's ears must surely have burst into flames—if there were any truth in the old adage.

When they got home Gordon Searle had met them at the airport, and Yvonne had rushed straight into the tale of misfortune, not giving Laurel a chance to speak, and furnished a somewhat highly coloured version of the unsuccessful mission that had made her father's mouth twitch.

'You did very well to get yourselves actually into the *castillo*,' he commented when he could get a word in edgeways. 'How did you manage it?'

'Our fatal charm—what did you think?' his daughter told him pertly. Then she caught Laurel's strained glance and lowered her voice. 'Actually, Daddy, poor Laurie had a frightful shock one night just after we arrived and it was the Conde himself who rescued her.' Yvonne hurried on with a highly dramatised account of the 'shock', which, however, was very craftily censored to omit any mention of her own part in the affair.

Gordon Searle's expression grew concerned. 'Is this true, my dear?' he asked. 'Yvonne isn't exaggerating?'

'I don't!' squealed Yvonne, and Laurel sighed. 'More or less,' she admitted, knowing she could do little but leave things as they stood if she were not to risk getting Yvonne into her parents' black books. 'Oh, Mr Searle, I'm so sorry!' she burst out. 'I've made a complete mess of everything and——'

'Nonsense! You couldn't help it.' He patted her shoulder consolingly. 'Not to worry—you can't win 'em all, you know.' He had carried them off to a splendid meal, after picking up Mrs Searle, who was now fully recovered and looking fit and well, and had launched into details of new plans for a holiday development in one of the as yet untouched Caribbean islands. As far as he was concerned Destino was written off as a non-starter and no regrets wasted on the matter.

But none of it should have happened that way. Laurel stared into space, her eyes troubled. Oh, why had she been so stupid? She should have told the Conde the truth that very first evening at the *castillo*. All of the trouble would have been averted. And she should never have fallen in love with that arrogant, wonderful, irresistible grandee ...

'Cheer up! You look as——' Mr Searle stopped by her desk and checked his bantering tone as he saw the glisten of tears she could not hide in time. 'Honey, what's the matter?'

She shook her head wordlessly, and tried to regain composure. But her boss frowned. 'You're not still taking that Destino business to heart, are you?'

Again she gave the hopeless little motion of her head, but he was too shrewd to be fooled.

'I think you are—you've been depressed ever since you came back, and I think I know you well enough by now to judge,' he said flatly. 'Please try not to worry. I'd feel happier if you'd forget all about it, Laurel.'

Forget! How could she?

'You had a Spanish knife in your back, Laurel,' he said in the same flat tones. 'No one could win in those circumstances. Now promise me you'll not let it prey on your mind any more. Has Yvonne told you about her birthday party?'

'Yes,' Laurel blew her nose and blinked away the wateriness in her eyes. 'It's in three weeks' time. I was going to ask you if you know of anything she would especially like.'

'Well, the perfume department from Harrods for a start,' he said with such dry humour Laurel had to smile. 'Her list of present suggestions kicks off with tights and works up to a car—but she'll get the music centre she's yammered on about for ages and think herself lucky.' He paused and his face grew thoughtful. 'I must say she's much easier to get on with since the Destino trip. More approachable and less moody, an of course my wife's recovery has made a difference. She was so poorly she couldn't cope with Yvonne, got irritable and impatient with her, all of which aggravated matters. But everything's tremendously improved now, thank heaven.'

'I'm glad,' Laurel said with sincerity.

He smiled. 'I rather think I owe a great deal to you, my dear. She has formed a great admiration for you and I hope you'll stay her friend, even though I realise she's bound to seem a bit juvenile at times.'

The genuine sincerity behind the words brought a warmth to Laurel's still bruised heart. She said awkwardly, 'Of course—but I think Yvonne's juvenile moods have ended now.'

He laughed, and with a fatherly quip at his daughter's expense moved towards his office, leaving Laurel to reflect on his remarks. At least her kindly employer's domestic troubles seemed to have ironed themselves out at last and for that she was thankful. If only she could say the same of her own! If only she didn't have this constant ache nagging at her conscience as well as her heart.

Although the hurt left by the Conde's merciless dismissal still felt as raw as ever she could not escape the guilty knowledge of her own quota of responsibility for what had happened. Had the positions been reversed how would she have felt if she had welcomed someone into her home only to discover that they came with an ulterior purpose? She would have felt angry and disappointed. It was no use trying to avoid this truth by pleading the conflict of circumstances out of her control; Yvonne's youthful folly and her own loyalty to her employer. The basic truth remained exactly the same when stripped of other considerations; she hadn't behaved very well.

But what was the use of worrying about it now? Laurel sighed deeply. She had sunk her pride and written to him the week after her return, apologising for the deception and thanking him for his kindness to herself and Yvonne. It had not been an easy letter to write and she had half filled her waste-paper basket before she succeeded in saying what she wanted to convey without any dangerous betrayal of emotional feeling. It had taken quite a bit of courage to post the epistle and the temptation to crumple it impatiently and fling it away had remained even as she hesitated at the pillar box. Of course it wouldn't make any difference, she told herself scornfully; he had made it perfectly plain what he thought of her, but at least she had done what her aunt would call the right thing and all she could do now was start the long, painful business of forgetting.

Despite this resolution Laurel could not suppress the forlorn hope that he might acknowledge her letter, but as the weeks passed this gradually withered and she tried to harden herself against such weakness.

Yvonne's birthday party came and went, after a noisy, hectic party that went on until the small hours of the next day, and the long summer days stretched ahead, filled with promise for that young lady but strangely remote from any joy for Laurel. It was as though something precious had gone from her capacity for living. Two men came into her life that summer, one of whom she met at Yvonne's party and the other who was a newcomer to Mr Searle's staff. They both made overtures of interest, but no matter how she tried to accept the warm dawn of new relationships the chill of remoteness deep within her refused to melt.

'I'm getting worried about you,' Yvonne exclaimed bluntly one afternoon in late July when she called in at the office. 'You're just wasting away this gorgeous summer. What's the matter?'

'Nothing. I've been rather busy, you know,' Laurel evaded with a smile.

'Rubbish! Daddy isn't such a slave-driver, is he?'

'I never said he was—whatever put that idea into your head?'

'Dunno—but it's got to be something.' Yvonne looked worried. 'Listen, Laurie, I'd rather you told me—it's not me, is it? I mean, I don't bore you. Only

I thought you'd like to see our weekend cottage, and that dress show last week was quite fun.'

Laurel gaped. For a moment she did not know what to say. Then Yvonne rushed on: 'I suddenly remembered that I said a few bitchy things to you when we first went to Destino and I wondered if you were still sort of annoyed about them. I mean,' she bit her lip, 'you don't have to be polite to me just because my father's your boss. And I didn't mean it, you know. I was going through a bad patch then and everything——'

'Oh, Yvonne—no!' Laurel recovered from astonishment. 'How could you think ... Of course you don't bore me. I loved that weekend with your parents and you at the cottage. If it hadn't been for all these invitations I'd have felt very out of things.'

'Thank God for that! Phew! As long as it isn't my fault!' Yvonne visibly relaxed, but a slight frown still puckered her brow. 'Then what is it? Have you fallen out with Phil?'

'Phil?' Laurel almost burst out laughing. Suddenly she realised she had not given a thought to Phil since her return. Heavens! Was it only three months since Phil walked out of her life and left her to cry herself to sleep? Phil, who had occupied all her waking dreams for a whole six months. An ironic smile curved her mouth. If she could forget one man so easily there was hope for her!

'What's so funny?'

'I'm sorry.' Laurel's face sobered. 'No, it isn't Phil. How did you know about him, anyway?'

'Oh, Daddy mentioned him just last night. He said he once or twice took a call from Phil at the office and he used to call for you sometimes, but he hadn't noticed him around lately.'

'It's over. We ended it three months ago.'

'That's ancient history!' Yvonne pushed her long thick hair back from her face, muttering that she must get it cut. 'Well, listen, Laurie, I came to see if you were doing anything tonight. I know it's short notice, but

you remember Noel—*okay*! I know he doesn't turn
you on—well, his brother has just come back from
Egypt and we're going to a new place that's just opened
—they say it's the last word and super food—and we
want you to meet Rick. Sandy and Clive are coming
as well.'

'A blind date? Or are you trying to matchmake
again?'

'Of course not!' Yvonne looked indignant. 'Sandy's
met Rick—before he went to Egypt—and she says he's
gorgeous. Oh, please, Laurie—it'll be fun.'

'All right.' Laurel capitulated, unable to resist all
this persuasion. 'Is it jeans, or ethnic, or full evening
splendour?'

'Oh, wear that lovely misty floating thing you bought
for my party. It'll be perfect. I bet Rick will fall for
you like a load of bricks!'

With this prophecy Yvonne departed for the hairdresser, after arranging to call for Laurel at eight
o'clock that evening. When she had gone Laurel was
left with a sudden sense of pleasureable anticipation, a
feeling she had not experienced for some time, and
by the time she let herself into her flat shortly after five
she was really looking forward to the evening ahead.
For once she was going to forget a tall man whose eyes
could caress like warm dark velvet and whose passionate mouth could make her whole body dissolve into
longing. But those same eyes could burn like a brand,
she reminded herself bitterly, and that mouth was
capable of shrivelling her with its scorn and arrogance.
Yes, tonight was going to mark the end of memories
and the start of forgetting.

She closed the door with unwonted force, as though
it were a symbolic underlining of new resolution, and
went to make herself a quick cup of tea. Unfortunately
her hairdresser had regretted that he was unable to fit
her in at such short notice so she would have to have a
shampoo and fix it herself. She would wear those
dainty new undies snapped up at a sale she'd gone to
with Yvonne last week, and she would open that new

perfume she'd been hoarding since Christmas. She had just pinned up fragrant, newly washed hair and was running her bath when the phone rang.

Thank heaven it hadn't waited till she was in the bath!

She hurried to answer, and her heart plummeted when she heard Yvonne's voice at the other end of the line. Oh, surely the evening wasn't off! She breathed her relief when Yvonne said quickly: 'I thought I'd better warn you—I'll be a bit earlier. Something's cropped up and Daddy has to see a client, so he'll have to be back before eight-thirty. But he's going to run us over to Sandy's place and then we can go on with them. Can you be ready?'

'Yes, of course—no bother.'

'Goody—see you about twenty to. By-eee!'

Laurel glanced at the clock as she turned away from the telephone. She still had the best part of a couple of hours; no need to rush over the luxurious bath she'd promised herself, with lashings of the rich golden bubbly stuff that made one relax deliciously, then the sensuously scented body lotion that Phil had once bought for her—with rather more sensuous ideas in mind. It was the first time she had ever been propositioned by a man and she had promptly handed him back the expensive flagon of lotion. But he had just laughed and said he had no intention of rushing her, trying to kid her he'd only been kidding . . . Well, there was no sense in leaving the stuff to decorate the bathroom shelf, she reflected wryly as she slipped into her robe and went through to the bathroom.

She selected her choice of garments, checked that a new pair of tights were flaw-free, and spread them carefully over the bed, then sat down at the dressing table to lacquer her nails. While they dried she would be cooling off from the bath. Ten minutes later she was holding pearl-tipped fingers under the cold water tap to complete the hardening when she heard the door bell.

She exclaimed under her breath. Surely it couldn't

be Yvonne already? It was still scarcely past seven. Or had her watch stopped? But the clock in the living room confirmed the watch's verdict as she ran to the door.

'Yvonne, you're soon! I'm not—*Oh*!'

But it was not Yvonne.

The door latch slipped away from Laurel's fingers and she caught at the edge to steady herself as she stared at her visitor. It couldn't be! She was seeing things!

'Good evening, *señorita*.'

She wasn't seeing a ghost! Laurel opened her mouth weakly then closed it and swallowed hard. '*Señor ...?*' she whispered incredulously.

'You are surprised to see me? I come in reply to your letter,' the Conde said calmly, his glance dropping briefly to her hands where they were clutching the tie belt of her robe. 'But I fear I have chosen an inopportune moment. Forgive me. I will return later, *señorita*.'

He was preparing to turn away, and something came to urgent life in Laurel, overcoming the tremors of agitation pulsating through her veins. She put out her hand. 'No, don't go—I'm going out soon. I—I never expected to see——' She was caught and held by his gaze as he turned back and her voice deserted her. She could only drown in the sight of him and step back mutely.

He paused for an instant on the threshold, and again his eyes strayed to the nervous hand fluttering to secure the edges of the robe at her throat. A nerve throbbed at the corner of his mouth. 'You trust me, *señorita*?'

'Shouldn't I?' she managed shakily.

'*Dios mio!*' He closed his eyes despairingly as he slammed shut the door behind him. 'Will I ever understand you? Even if I were betrothed to a girl of my own people I would never be permitted to glimpse her attired as you are at this moment—let alone be left alone with her.'

'But I'm not of your people, and I'm not betrothed

to you.' Laurel strove to keep her voice steady. 'Anyway, I can't stand at the door like this, so if you could wait—while I dress——' his eyes were making a fiasco of all her earlier resolution—— 'I'll only be a few minutes and then——'

'No—wait, Laurel.' He took a step forward. 'Tell me, why did you write to me?'

'Why?' she stared at him, then shrugged. 'Because I felt guilty, I suppose.'

'That was all?'

'Wasn't it enough?'

'No.' He shook his head slowly, and the negative was heavy with finality. Laurel's mouth tightened and her chin went up. 'Listen, *señor*,' she began firmly. 'I tried to explain in my letter that I never intended to deceive you about the reason I came to Destino. But the way things happened I couldn't—not until it was too late and we were actually at the *castillo*. And then——'

'Yes?' he prompted.

'I couldn't, because . . .' She turned away hopelessly. What was the use of starting all the anguish again? How could she explain without betraying her heart?

'Loyalty to your employer, perhaps?' he broke in.

'Something like that,' she said dully.

'But you did not believe I would listen courteously to the truth? Even if I had to refuse your request?'

'Well, would you?' she cried. 'Everything I did seemed to anger you! And the night of the *romeria*, after Carlota told you, I tried to explain and apologise, but you wouldn't listen. You just grew about ten feet tall and looked down at me as if—as if I——' Her voice broke and she gulped in a ragged breath. 'You seemed to forget that it was your own idea that we stay at the *castillo*—you insisted on it! It was to suit your own purpose in the first place, and then you practically threw us out. That was what it amounted to,' she accused hotly.

'Yes—but did I not have good cause?' The familiar rapier points glowed in the dark eyes. 'You had given me your kisses, melted in my arms as though you desired me. Was it not all part of your plan of deceit while you spied out my home and my island? I believed you an innocent when I looked into your eyes and sensed the tender wakening of your body to awareness of me, while all the time you seemed to fight that awakening. And when Carlota told me the truth I could scarcely believe you capable of such duplicity. I——'

'No!' Dawning horror widened Laurel's eyes. 'It wasn't like that! You can't believe that I—that I deliberately let you make love to me because I—Oh, no! It was because of Yvonne and her father—my boss —and she was frightened of more trouble.' Laurel took a deep breath, not realising that she had put an imploring hand on his arm as she poured out the story of Yvonne's involvement with unsavoury companions, the drug fear, her mother's illness and Gordon Searle's worry, probably the real motive behind Gordon Searle's dispatching of the two girls to Destino. 'I don't think he was really bothered about Destino from a business angle,' she rushed on frantically, desperate that the Conde should understand. 'And then Yvonne got involved with Renaldo and he took her ring, which was very valuable, that her father had given her. She was just beginning to come to her senses and realise how much distress she'd caused, and then that happened. She begged me not to risk our getting sent back home because you'd found out. And her father would never do anything unethical. I'm sure now that he was just trying to make me feel I was doing something useful to justify a long holiday at his expense. Because he wasn't in the least bit angry when we got back and told him I'd failed. But you must not believe that I— that I would use my sex to deceive you. It's not true!'

For a long moment he did not speak, and Laurel could scarcely bear the probing gaze that seemed to search down into her soul. Then he said softly: 'So, if that were not true, why could you not explain all this much sooner?'

She looked away, running trembling fingers over the soft little mounds of pinned-up hair.

'Was I so unapproachable?' he persisted.

She found the wisp straying free of its pin and doggedly pressed it back into place. 'It wasn't easy to explain things to you,' she said, refusing to look at him.

'Even when you were in my arms?'

She gave an imperceptible little shake of her head, and the silence stretched unbearably into a spell she could not break. The clock's tick became noticeable, heightening the tension of stillness in the room, and then, so suddenly that she started nervously, the Conde uttered a sharp exclamation.

'Laurel, *amada mia*—someone once said that silence and solitude are as death to a Spaniard. I think it is true! One thing I do know: I can not face a future without the sound of your voice and the presence of your sweet, intractable, tantalising self.'

'W-what?' Laurel froze, wondering if she had heard aright. She looked for the glints of mockery in his dark eyes and looked in vain.

'*Si!* Stop looking at me as though you doubt both my sanity and your own. And tell me you wrote that letter because you cared about my opinion of you.'

'I think you know that already,' she murmured weakly.

'*Si!* But I want to hear you say it!'

Still she did not dare believe what her clamouring senses were telling her, nor what an age-old instinct urged her do. 'It's weeks since I wrote that letter,' she evaded. 'You didn't even answer.'

'Because the letter was delayed in a postal dispute, and by the time it reached the *castillo* I had gone away —to try to fill a certain gap which had disturbingly appeared in my life. When it finally came into my hands I decided to respond in person.' He paused, a wicked glint coming into his eyes. 'I believed you needed my forgiveness, *señorita*.'

'*Your* forgiveness!' She was still trying to resist belief, subduing the incredulous joy that wanted to bubble up and overflow. 'What about mine? For the way you looked and spoke to me that night. Always angry. Always ready to accuse. Except when——'

'Except when I could not resist desire a moment longer? Is that what you are trying to tell me but are too shy?' He gave an exclamation that was halfway between laughter and despair. 'Oh, Laurie *mia*! When will you begin to understand our temperament? That when we feel anger we have to voice it? We cannot hide our feelings, just as we cannot conceal our ardour or remain cold in our attitude for very long. *Si*, we quarrel, often hurt, but when it is over we do not bear malice. And the exchanging of forgiveness can be very sweet.'

He moved towards her, his hands taking hers and drawing her to stand close in front of him. 'Shall we seal this forgiveness once and for all, and then . . .?'

His arms went round her, settling her against him, and he kissed her, lightly, sweetly, and then with a deepening intensity that betrayed his hunger. Long moments later he whispered, 'I will not pretend that there will not be times when I will be angry, and you will be angry, *querida*, and we will quarrel, but you will always know that it is because you have the power to hurt and invoke anger. If I did not care I would be indifferent.' He moved his mouth against hers, tasting her lips in a sensuous caress that went to Laurel's head like a potent wine. But she forced herself to draw back and look up into his eyes, now unfathomably deep with his ardour.

'You're not going to marry Carlota?'

'Carlota? Heaven forbid! Where did you get that idea?' His brows narrowed, then relaxed with resignation. 'I know—Abuelita has been talking to you. But there is no arrangement, do not fear. And you?' his voice sharpened, 'you are going out tonight—with a man? If so, you will cancel it. You will make no more dates with any other man from now onwards. You are mine! And I shall never allow you to forget that fact. Is that clear?'

'More or less.' Laurel stretched up her arms and surrendered to the bliss of enfolding them round his neck and resting her cheek against the smooth, warm male-fragrant skin. 'There is just one thing ...'

'I know ...' his lips found the lobe of her ear, 'I have not officially made a proposal of marriage. Will you marry me, Señorita Laurel Daneway, and be my Condesa of Castillo Valderosa?'

'Oh, yes!' she sighed in a whisper.

'Say my name. And tell me you love me.'

'I love you—so much I can't believe it's true. I'm afraid to wake up—Rodrigo, *amado*,' she whispered.

'It is no dream—I will prove it.' He crushed her to him, his passion riding high now and carrying her with him on a wild sweet surge of ecstasy. Like wisps of mist at dawn all the unhappiness of the past few weeks melted and were gone. Laurel forgot her surroundings, forgot everything, even the scantiness of her attire that was all too frail a barrier between her glowing body and the hard male hunger of his—until he gave a groan of torment and buried his mouth in the warm hollow of her neck.

'No, *querida mía*—not yet, alas.' His breathing came quick and uneven, then slowly steadied as he fought down the tumult of desire. His arms slackened. 'I think you had better put on some clothing or I will not be responsible for my actions.'

But he still held her, reluctantly putting her at arms-length while Laurel tried to break free of the ecstasy that held her a willing captive.

'Do you remember the first time we met?' he asked huskily.

The lovely rose tinted her cheeks and she nodded.

'I was too angered by your foolhardy obstinacy that day to be aroused by your unclad body. But now, in memory ...' He looked at her, the unfinished evocation saying more than any words ever could. Slowly he raised his head and drew aside the lapel of her robe, bending his head. Just once his mouth touched the silken softness of her breast, infinitely tender, caressed and adored its dusky bud, then he drew the veil across temptation and thrust her gently away.

'Temptation and tradition make poor bedfellows,' he sighed regretfully. 'Now do as I bid you.'

'Or I will be punished?' she whispered mischievously.

'Or you will be punished.'

'I hope you're not going to banish me behind the traditional grille, to flutter my eyelashes and a lace fan while we complete our courtship?' she asked with pretended dismay.

'That may be necessary, unless you marry me very soon, my little paragon of virtue,' he said, brows quirking wickedly so that she laughed softly with pure joy.

He frowned. 'You may well laugh—no one at this moment except myself would believe you either a paragon or virtuous. It is as well that I am not totally without the ability to judge a woman's true character,' he added with imperious self-assurance.

But he caught her hand as she would have turned away, and the expression in his eyes made her heart turn over with a welling of love that was a sweet pain.

'Tempt me with just one more kiss—before I submit to the discipline of tradition,' he said softly.

For a moment Laurel gazed at him and her eyes took on a remote light. This was the velvet touch, but she had no illusions about the sheer feline power, the fire and the steel behind those burning magnetic eyes and the handsome chiselled features. No woman would ever tame this man—and she knew in her heart that she had no desire to be the one who would ever attempt to emasculate that fiery spirit. It was enough that he should love her . . .

With a heartfelt little cry she ran to be caught close and melt within his arms, surrendering to the blaze of desire in his dark eyes and giving herself up to this prelude to all the ecstasy to come.

She scarcely heard the doorbell ring, and ring, and ring . . .

What a surprise for Yvonne!

The Warrender Saga

The most frequently requested series of Harlequin Romances . . . Mary Burchell's Warrender Saga

A Song Begins   The Curtain Rises
The Broken Wing   Song Cycle
Child of Music   Music of the Heart
Unbidden Melody
Remembered Serenade
When Love Is Blind

Each complete novel is set in the exciting world of music and opera, spanning the years from the meeting of Oscar and Anthea in *A Song Begins* to his knighthood in *Remembered Serenade*. These nine captivating love stories introduce you to a cast of characters as vivid, interesting and delightful as the glittering, exotic locations. From the tranquil English countryside to the capitals of Europe— London, Paris, Amsterdam—the Warrender Saga will sweep you along in an unforgettable journey of drama, excitement and romance.

Complete and mail this coupon today!

Remember when a good love story made you feel like holding hands?

The wonder of love is timeless. Once discovered, love remains, despite the passage of time. Harlequin brings you stories of true love, about women the world over – women like you.

Harlequin Romances with the Harlequin magic...

Recapture the sparkle of first love... relive the joy of true romance... enjoy these stories of love today.

Six new novels every month – wherever paperbacks are sold.